TIME LOCK 2:
THE KYOTO CONSPIRACY

TIME
LOCK 2:
THE KYOTO CONSPIRACY

HOWARD BERK
AND
PETER BERK

IE Snaps
by
IngramElliott

Published by IngramElliott, Inc.
www.ingramelliott.com
9815-J Sam Furr Road, Suite 271, Huntersville, NC 28078

Book formatting by Creative Publishing Book Design
Cover design by H.O. Charles
Editing by Katherine Bartis

ISBN Paperback: 978-1-952961-18-2
ISBN E-Book: 978-1-952961-19-9

Library of Congress Control Number: 2023939687

Subjects: Fiction—Action and Adventure. Fiction—Thrillers—Suspense. Fiction—Science Fiction—General.

Published in the United States of America. Printed in the United States of America.

First Edition: 2023, First International Edition: 2023

The *TimeLock* series by
Howard Berk and Peter Berk

A sci-fi-tinged action-adventure with heart and humor, the *TimeLock* series is set in the crime-ridden near future where a bold new technology transforms the justice system and challenges America's moral compass. Only one problem—what happens if you're innocent?

TimeLock

When everyman Morgan Eberly is arrested for a murder he didn't commit, he's subjected to an experimental new technology that instantly ages prisoners the number of years of their sentence. Now forty-three and on the run, can Morgan and rogue FBI agent Janine Price unlock the truth about TimeLock before it's too late to turn back?

TimeLock 2: The Kyoto Conspiracy

Two years after the events of *TimeLock*, Morgan Eberly and Janine Price are forced to journey from DC to Japan to Siberia to prevent the development of a new weaponized form of TimeLock authorized by the unhinged and deadly new president of the United States.

Coming Soon

TimeLock 3

The exciting next chapter of the *TimeLock* series.

Dedication

To my beloved family—my wife, Diane,
our sons Jordan and Daniel, our grandchildren Aiden,
Dylan, and Daphne, and our daughters-in-law
Stephanie and Rosi. And, as always and forever,
to my cherished father and mother, Howard and Lynn.

ACKNOWLEDGMENTS

As before, my profound thanks to the warm, wise, and wonderful team at IngramElliott, who made all of my professional dreams come through with their support, kindness, and guidance and who let me "collaborate" once again with my favorite author—my dad, Howard Berk.

PROLOGUE

MAY 12, 2034, KYOTO, JAPAN

Right on cue, the sedan chasing us appears in my rearview mirror. I have to make this next piece convincing, so I start weaving the car around as we climb up the winding road toward the summit. Even Janine can't hold back a scream or two, but I don't let up—this has to be believable.

A minute later, we turn another curve and are out of our pursuer's line of sight. I slow the car down.

"Everybody out!"

Now Janine gets it. I turn the wheel toward the edge of the road as the three of us burst out of the car and scramble behind some trees. A moment later, the sedan approaches just in time to see our car fly off the side of the road and soar a thousand feet to a virtually inaccessible crevice below. Unlike in the movies, the car doesn't randomly burst into flames on its way down or even when it crashes, but nobody looking at the crumpled heap of metal below would think for a second that there were any survivors.

The two men in the sedan—just far enough from us that we can't make out their faces—get out and look over the edge, clearly satisfied with a job well done. They get back in the sedan, turn it around, and drive back toward Kyoto.

Yoshi, Janine, and I give each other relieved hugs, then Yoshi turns to me and says, "Thank you, Morgan. You saved our lives."

"Your idea, Yoshi."

"Let's call it teamwork. What matters is we're still alive!"

I squeeze his shoulder, smile, and say what any James Bond fan who just faked his own death would say, especially in Japan of all places.

"You only live twice."

CHAPTER ONE

FOUR DAYS EARLIER, WASHINGTON, DC

Two years ago, I was twenty years younger. My name is Morgan Eberly, and if you know my story, you also know that such a mathematical impossibility can only be explained by one word: TimeLock.

If you don't know my story, let me briefly recap it for you. But I should warn you in advance—if you like your narratives to fit squarely into a single genre, mine may not be for you. The reason is simple: what I experienced back in 2032 was part mystery, part thriller, part tragedy, and even part comedy (of errors, thanks to me).

Happily, though, in the end my story was mainly an epic romance revolving around two wholly disparate people who first meet as enemies of sorts, gradually bond over a shared social injustice (not to mention multiple attempts on their lives), discover how much they actually love each other, and then, against all odds, begin to live happily ever after.

It all began with the murder of my friend, Lonny Myers, who had recently been arrested for robbery and was unfortunately among the very first to be processed through a radical new prison program called TimeLock. Promoted by Myra Winters, then governor of my home state of Maryland, TimeLock—created by a genetics company called Genescence—represented a hugely controversial attempt to tackle two of the most prevalent social issues of the time: rampant crime and prison overcrowding.

The concept was as simple as the science was complex. Through the terrifying marvels of instant genetic acceleration, prisoners would be aged the number of years of their sentence in a matter of minutes rather than serving conventional time. A month-long recovery phase would then kick in, after which the older and hopefully wiser inmates would be free to rejoin polite society.

For a short period of time, TimeLock admittedly achieved its dual objectives of scaring potential criminals straight and ensuring that convicted criminals who went through the program wouldn't so much as jaywalk once they were free. But then, in what would constitute an almost laughable irony if it wasn't so deadly serious, it turned out that the TimeLock program itself had more wrinkles than any of the unfortunate prisoners who were processed through it.

More specifically, some of the initial inmates who went through began to suddenly age into oblivion not long after their release. Desperate to protect his company's multi-billion-dollar government contract, Genescence CEO Patrick Loder therefore began systematically eliminating the afflicted prisoners, including the aforementioned Lonny Myers, careful not only to make their deaths all appear to be accidents, but to ensure the bodies were never found and examined.

And that's where I came into the picture. Having arranged to meet up with Lonny for the first time since he had gotten out of prison, I found myself witness to his brutal murder by two assailants. Within hours, I was wrongly arrested for that murder and then—still at the tender age of twenty-three—given a forty-year sentence to be carried out through TimeLock within days.

Like Lonny and a few dozen others before me, I soon found myself strapped inside a TimeLock capsule being assaulted by a veritable tsunami of terrifying chemicals, gases, gamma rays, and God knows what else, all working in tandem to steal away precious years of my life with every passing second.

Miraculously, however, while I was in the middle of being processed, dozens of civilians protesting against TimeLock overwhelmed the facility and temporarily brought operations to a halt. With the guards distracted by the invading crowd, I was able to break out of my capsule, blend in with the protesters, and eventually escape altogether.

Best of all—relatively speaking—I quickly discovered I had only been aged half of my sentence. Coping with the sudden arrival of middle age was an emotional and physical ordeal I'm still trying to wrap my head around two years later, but having avoided joining the AARP set that fateful morning is something I continue to thank the heavens for every day.

After my escape, I was frightened and alone, holed up in dingy motels, subsisting on cheap takeout, pursued by the cops and Lonny's killers, and shunned by even my closest friends. Knowing I couldn't spend the rest of my newly curtailed life on the run, I decided to reach out to the one person I knew with the authority to help me: Janine Price, the very same FBI agent who had arrested me in the first place.

While I knew Janine was no fan of TimeLock herself, I wasn't surprised that by-the-book Agent Price wanted no part of harboring an escaped prisoner like myself—even if it meant uncovering the truth about the program and Loder's deadly cover-up.

Eventually, however, a combination of the facts and my undeniable charm (please don't repeat this to Janine—she'll deny the part about my charm!), convinced even the skeptical Janine that I had been right all along. So, a tenuous partnership was formed, one which almost cost Janine her life's work and almost cost both of us our actual lives, but which eventually brought Loder and Genescence down in flames and Janine and I together for good.

Soon after, the FBI was able to prove I had been innocent in Lonny's killing after all. At long last, I was a free man. More than that, I was a changed man. Before all this, I had been something of an emotional drifter, unable to ever be fully at ease with myself, much less settle down with someone else. But thanks to Janine's support, and, oddly enough, thanks to the passage of years forced upon me by TimeLock, I found myself not only filled with a sense of purpose and self-worth that had eluded me as long as I could remember, but ready to share my future with the love of my life. And we haven't looked back since.

Like I said—happily ever after.

CHAPTER TWO

I t's been nearly two years since I was processed through TimeLock. Meaning I'm now forty-five—and I feel it. My knees are touch and go, and I wear reading glasses now. And when Janine is in the next room, I sometimes watch TV with the subtitles on because I can't hear half of what they're saying.

But minor ailments aside, I'm in pretty good shape. Swimming helps, and I'm at the gym three times a week. And nothing compares to taking my new Yahama Bolt motorcycle out for a spin on the weekends. Truth be told, Janine isn't too wild about my weekend warrior proclivities, but then again, I worry about her every day she heads off to work at the FBI, ready to bring down the Patrick Loders of the world.

Best of all, Janine and I have been living together for well over a year, and I plan on making that arrangement permanent soon. There isn't a person on the planet who knows less about engagement rings, but I'll do my best not to embarrass myself. That said, if you hear a woman laughing hysterically in a DC condo about a month from now, you'll know I blew it.

What continues to amaze me the most about my relationship with Janine—other than the fact that she still hasn't come to her senses and kicked me out—is how much we've changed each other for the better along the way. Before my nightmarish association with TimeLock first began, I was the polar opposite of Janine in just about every conceivable way: smart but hardly wise, easily distracted, professionally unambitious, emotionally immature, and only able to commit to "relationships" that could be measured in hours or days.

By contrast, Janine grew up in a highly disciplined family devoted to law enforcement and knew from an early age exactly what she'd do with her life. As a result, the Janine I met two years ago was grounded well beyond her years, focused, driven, and so defined by her career as an FBI agent that I was surprised she didn't wear her badge to bed at night.

Somewhere along the way, though, our personalities started to meet more in the middle, and today, I'm not sure we would recognize or particularly like the people we were before TimeLock brought us together. For my part, two years of admiring a woman as self-assured, in control, and morally centered as Janine has changed me in ways I never would have thought possible not that long ago. How else do you explain that the same man who once thought no further than tonight's beer or tomorrow's motorcycle ride is now running his own relatively prosperous cybersecurity consulting business, can't wait to get married, and is even thinking about becoming a father someday?

For her part, I think Janine has learned a thing or two from me as well, like how to embrace the freewheeling, spontaneous, and even silly side of herself she had kept dormant for so long. And how to not only go by the book in her work, but to sometimes write a boldly original new chapter for that book as well—much as she did when she abandoned all caution to help an escaped convict by the name of Morgan Eberly bring down the deadly TimeLock program.

As healthy as our personal relationship is now, however, Janine and I can't help but worry about the health of the country these days. The reason is simple: to no political prognosticator's surprise, Myra Winters is now president of the United States. True, our new commander in chief hasn't mentioned her beloved TimeLock once since announcing her candidacy, but that hardly means she won't resuscitate it in the future.

Put simply, even though I've escaped prison and escaped more attempts on my life than I care to remember, I can't escape the nagging feeling that, to paraphrase Mark Twain, reports of TimeLock's death have been greatly exaggerated. Especially given the conversation then Governor Winters had with former President William Bartlett in which she supposedly espoused an insane and illegal plan to weaponize TimeLock in order to cause instant cellular degradation among enemy combatants.

How that would work exactly, I haven't a clue. Wouldn't it violate every ban on chemical warfare that exists throughout the civilized world? And even if it did work somehow, wouldn't enemy nations simply switch to dropping bombs instead of arming soldiers? But those are logical questions a sane person would ask and I'm increasingly worried sanity and Myra Winters filed for divorce and took up separate residences a long time ago.

Leaving me to wonder uneasily just what she's really up to behind the Oval Curtain.

If anything is keeping Americans up at night now, though, it's the increasing possibility of a war breaking out between the United States and North Korea. Dear leader Kim Il Kwan is truly certifiable, the most unstable and barbarous dictator to ever rule that cursed nation. Maybe he and our president should be fitted with matching straightjackets.

In any case, North Korea is why Janine and I are so concerned about our dear friends who live in Kyoto, Japan—Dr. Lionel Garvey and his wife Anna. If North Korea acts on its threat to launch a "thunderstorm of missiles" over the Sea of Japan, Kyoto might well be one of its first targets.

It was the sixty-five-year-old Dr. Garvey who had— against his will—been forced to develop the TimeLock process. Though I initially despised him for having indirectly stolen twenty years from me, I eventually learned he had been as much of a victim of Patrick Loder's murderous reign as I was. And then came a true shocker. The night Genescence burned to the ground and Patrick Loder died, Dr. Garvey told me he had been the first to test TimeLock early in its development but the experiment was a disastrous failure: instead of aging himself a couple of years, he accidentally was aged a full thirty years instead.

Like two overcooked peas in a pod, Dr. Garvey and I suddenly shared a bond like no other—two young men forced to somehow adjust to the instantaneous loss of precious decades of their lives. Decades I assumed we could never get back. Until, that is, Dr. Garvey uttered a sentence I've replayed in my mind a thousand times over the past two years: "There may be a way back for both of us."

I didn't push him on it then, and in fact haven't heard anything further about this possible godsend since, even though I'm tempted every day to ask him if he's made any progress since that fateful night. Still, I know if and when Dr. Garvey does find a "cure"—a way to actually reverse the original TimeLock process—I'll be the first to find out.

CHAPTER THREE

Now comes the part of my story you *don't* know. Soon after discovering the unfortunate bond Dr. Garvey and I shared, Janine and I realized we wanted to learn what we could about his background and what led him to be an unwitting pawn in Patrick Loder's homicidal rampage. But it was more than mere curiosity. We genuinely liked Dr. Garvey and his wife Anna and even identified with them. After all, here was another unlikely couple that had been tested to the core by TimeLock, yet had emerged stronger than ever in the aftermath.

Which is why I suggested we invite the Garveys to spend a weekend at my family's newly rebuilt mountain cabin in Thurmont, Maryland, last year. Yes, the very same cabin Loder's assassins burned down after killing Lonny Myers. Now, you're probably thinking exactly what Janine was when I first broached the idea: Is he insane? This was, after all, where I witnessed a murder that I was eventually convicted of and where my horrifying association with TimeLock first began.

To make matters worse, Janine needlessly reminded me, I'd be revisiting this repository of traumatic memories and lost years with the very man who created TimeLock in the first place.

Much to Janine's surprise, though, I looked at things rather differently. Sure, I knew going back there would churn up dark memories, but what if, conversely, it turned out to instead be the ideal opportunity for a long overdue catharsis? The chance to rise like a phoenix from the ashes of the past and stand tall in the light of a hopeful new future—much like the once-burned-down cabin itself.

And so we went, and I was right; it proved to be one of the most cathartic experiences of my life. What I didn't foresee is how bittersweet it was to return to our family cabin with a man old enough to be my father. Of course, my own father, a tech genius who traveled the world, had been gone for almost a decade, and Lionel, despite his benevolent grandfatherly appearance, was really a man under forty trapped in the ultimate unwanted disguise. Yet still, it was sometimes impossible not to look at him that weekend and think of my real father and the life that might have been had he not died in a tragic train derailment in China.

That first evening, laughter, tears, and wine all flowed in equal measure. And there was surprise as well on our part. Starting with the reminder that Lionel Garvey's real name wasn't Lionel Garvey at all, it was Louis Garrett. As he told us that clear, crisp starry night, the death of his parents at relatively young ages sparked his professional calling: he would become the twenty-first-century equivalent of Ponce de Leon and find a way to slow, perhaps even to temporarily reverse, the aging process.

Several years and multiple Harvard Medical School degrees later, Louis was where he was meant to be—Japan, a global bastion of human longevity. And it was at a reception in Kyoto when he first saw her—the most beautiful woman he had ever laid eyes on. Shy by nature, Louis could only marvel at this angelic vision from afar. But circumstance brought them together nonetheless when they both headed to the buffet line at the same time and struck up a conversation.

In her early twenties, her name was Kiyoko Ito, and by the end of that magical evening, she and Louis were nothing less than spellbound.

As in any good love story, however, an obstacle soon appeared that threatened to destroy Louis and Kiyoko's happiness before it could even begin. It turned out that Kiyoko's father was hardly the laid-back textile manufacturer he claimed to be. He was instead a member of the Japanese mafia—the Yakuza. The bigger threat to Louis and Kiyoko's future, though, was a younger but more ascendant figure in the local Yakuza named Akimutsu Watanabe who had set his sights on Kiyoko from the moment they met the previous year.

Knowing they had to get away and start fresh back in America, Louis and Kiyoko left for Boston and were married a month later. But three weeks after returning from their honeymoon, on a night when Louis was working late in his genetics lab, Watanabe showed up, broke into their home, and threatened to kill Kiyoko if she didn't return to Japan with him. She started to back off, but he violently plowed toward her in the kitchen. In a blur of fear and panic, she grabbed a knife and when he tried to wrestle it from her, it plunged deep into his chest and he fell to the ground, dead.

Fearing the Yakuza would seek vengeance, Louis contacted a Department of Justice acquaintance named Don Loder, who promptly set him and Kiyoko up in the Witness Protection Program. Their new names were Dr. Lionel Garvey and Anna Warner Garvey.

Anna secured a translation position at the State Department and Dr. Garvey was invited to join a small genetics lab, which was one of the many diverse companies run by Don Loder's uber-ambitious son, Patrick. Two years later, Dr. Garvey created a breakthrough formulation that seemed to accelerate the rejuvenation process. Initial trials on lab animals went seamlessly, but unfortunately, Patrick Loder was running out of both money and patience.

Then fate intervened.

At a fundraising event one evening, Loder happened to overhear newly elected Maryland Governor Myra Winters talking about the dire problem of crime and prison overcrowding in her state and nationwide. A crazy idea popped into Loder's head: What if Dr. Garvey's rejuvenation process could be reversed? What if he could make people older? Something nobody in the world would ever want, right? Nobody, that is, except a government that would almost certainly pay any amount to frighten criminals into finding another line of work once and for all.

But there was one problem—Dr. Garvey wanted nothing to do with it. The next day, he stormed into Loder's office and resigned. Unfortunately, Loder wouldn't hear of it. In fact, he knew everything about Louis and Kiyoko, including, as Loder put it, her "killing an intruder in cold blood." A complete lie, of course, considering her actions were entirely in self-defense. But hardly information a rising star in the State Department or a respected geneticist would want made public.

Though only concerned about Kiyoko and not himself, Louis agreed to work on TimeLock under one condition: he would test it on himself first. Three months later, the process was finalized but the cost was great—thirty-two-year-old Louis Garrett had inadvertently transformed himself into sixty-two-year-old Lionel Garvey.

Dr. Garvey had paid a steep price but Patrick Loder and Myra Winters of course didn't care. At long last, they had what they so desperately wanted.

TimeLock was born.

CHAPTER FOUR

I t's been over a year since that weekend vacation and more than six months since Louis and Kiyoko moved back to Kyoto. A move sparked in great part by Louis's desire to resume his genetics research far from the TimeLock-obsessed American media and the painful memories associated with Genescence and Patrick Loder.

Who could have foreseen that Janine and I would be joining our friends in Japan within days? Only this time it would hardly be for a vacation.

Janine and I are on the couch talking. One of the countless things I love most about my girlfriend/hopefully soon-to-be-fiancée is that she shares my fondness for careening back and forth randomly between serious conversations about important world events and silly observations about *Seinfeld*-like minutiae. Right now, we're having one of our dopiest back-and-forths ever—a rundown of our greatest pet peeves in life.

As it turns out, Janine has three pet peeves at the top of her list: people who bring babies to the movies; airplane passengers who are able to fall asleep before takeoff; and servers in restaurants who repeatedly call their customers "you guys."

Not bad, I tell her. But I think I can top them all with this: "The 'text and vanish.'"

"The what and what now?" Janine asks.

"The 'text and vanish.' Let me set the stage. It's eleven in the morning and your friend Yvette LaFenoire sends you a text—"

"I don't have a friend named Yvette LaFenoire."

"You do now."

"Okay, what does my dear friend Yvette LaFenoire say in her text?"

"She says: *We still meeting for lunch today at noon?* You with me so far?"

Janine gives me a fake withering smile and says, "Thanks to all that FBI training, I think I can keep up."

"Good. So you read the text and immediately reply: *Sure. What restaurant?* But inexplicably, Yvette has suddenly gone missing. Somehow, someway, in the milliseconds between the time she sent her text and the time you responded, she simply disappeared. You wait and wait, but she's gone. Maybe she suddenly decided to hurl her phone out the window, or maybe she hopped on a flight back to Paris, but either way, Yvette has left the building. For some unknown reason, she's turned a simple lunch plan into an Agatha Christie mystery. She has, in fact, committed the dreaded 'text and vanish.'"

Janine smiles and shakes her head. "I see you've given this a great deal of thought."

"I have."

"Glad to see you're using your stratospherically high IQ to solve such pressing societal problems," she says mockingly.

"Thank you."

And with that, Janine again smiles and then heads into the kitchen. Seconds later, I hear my text ding. I assume it's Janine about to play a little 'text and vanish' joke on me, but what's on the screen is definitely no laughing matter: *My sister Kiyoko and Louis have been abducted! Don't know who has done this or why. Kiyoko said to contact you both when in trouble. With police now. Must go. Please do not call here. I will call you soon. Yoshi Ito.*

I get up to tell Janine about the text when she dashes in from the kitchen. She's holding her phone up to show me she's just received the same text.

"Did Kiyoko ever mention having a brother?" Janine asks.

"Yeah, I think so. Young guy, mid-twenties. I think he works on a farm in Osaka."

"Remember they told us about her father, the Yakuza?" asks Janine. "Maybe there's a connection."

"But that was all years ago, and her father is long gone. So why now?"

"Can't be money. She and Louis are hardly wealthy."

I try Louis's number. No answer. I send him a text as well. Again, nothing.

"Can you bring in the Bureau?" I ask.

"To work a case in Japan? Only with their government's consent, and right now, we don't even know if this is true. The whole thing could be a hoax. How do we know the text really came from her brother?"

"We track him down and confirm his identity."

"How?"

"We brought down a billion-dollar company in Washington. We can find a farmer in Osaka."

CHAPTER FIVE

E xcept we *can't* find a farmer in Osaka. We spend the next half hour looking, even using my many "computer genius" tricks of the trade along with Janine's FBI database, but have come up short. There are thousands of Yoshi Itos in Japan and hundreds of them are farmers, but no matches anywhere near Osaka.

But a few minutes later, "our" Yoshi Ito sends us a new text reading: *Still waiting for Chief Inspector. Can't speak yet. Happened four hours ago. Had just arrived for visit with Kiyoko & Louis when they were kidnapped. Took these photos of van. Only took her in the van. Took Louis in a separate car. Can you help?*

27

We look closely at the three photos. They all show the front of a van. In the first two, we can see what must be Kiyoko being shoved into the back seat. In the third shot, the vehicle is driving forward. Though we can't make out a license plate in any of the images, we can see Japanese writing on the side of the van.

A few searches later and we have our translation: Flower Delivery. Well, *that* narrows it down. Completely useless.

But then Agent Price shows why she's been such a rising star at the FBI all these years. She sends the clearest image Yoshi sent us to a colleague at the Bureau and asks her to enlarge it.

"What are you looking for?" I ask.

"Chassis number."

"Huh?"

"Japanese vehicles don't use VIN numbers like we do, but they do have identification."

For the millionth time, I try to reach Louis or Kiyoko while we wait for Janine's pal at the Bureau and for the millionth time, I throw the phone down in frustration.

A couple of minutes later, the enhanced image comes back. And at the bottom of the windshield on the passenger side of the white van is a chassis number.

My turn at the computer—hacking into our horrible boss's vehicle records used to be a regular pastime in my QuickRight Financial Services days.

Ten minutes later, I've tracked the van to Jeiso Flowers, but it turns out this particular flower company has wilted and gone out of business. But that could be good news—maybe their vans were sold off and we can figure out who bought this one.

Another fifteen minutes later, we do. It was purchased five days ago by one Sloane Whalen from Norfolk, Virginia. This whole thing is getting weirder by the minute. Our person of interest isn't just an American, but an American based a scant three and a half hours from Washington.

With a name like Sloane Whalen, it shouldn't be all that difficult to get info about him. And, sure enough, getting what we're looking for isn't hard at all. *Believing* it is the hard part.

Sloane Whalen turns out to be a woman, a retired colonel with the Department of Defense who rose under the leadership of Brigadier General Carter Prescott, and is currently a highly paid national security advisor to none other than President Myra Winters.

I do a deep dive into Sloane's background and we learn that she met our current commander in chief nine years ago when the then up-and-coming Maryland Senator Winters was on the appropriations committee for the Department of Defense. At the time, more than a few observers noted that there seemed to be an almost immediate connection between the two women. Possibly, some of the more salacious stories speculated, even an attraction. This despite Myra being old enough to be Sloane's mother.

One thing is clear, though, both were hawkishly devoted to national security, both had zero tolerance for weakness or incompetence, both would do anything in their power to support the military, and both feared that even the slightest hint of appeasement would invite decimation by any number of foreign adversaries.

Given their shared worldviews, including a palpable disdain for outgoing President Bartlett's "flacid" response to increasing threats from North Korea, it surprised nobody when President Winters brought Sloane on as a national security advisor. Indeed, by all accounts, the newly elected president was soon spending far more time with Sloane than with anyone else in her orbit, including her vice president, her chief of staff, and even her husband.

Perhaps the most revealing coverage I find about Sloane Whalen, however, is a fawning profile of her written during Myra Winters' presidential run. Not surprisingly, it's a military magazine artlessly called *Battle Seekers*, and if I was in the market for my very own short-range ballistic missile, I'd be filling out my subscription form right now.

I'll say this for the six-foot-tall Ms. Whalen: with her chiseled face and short-cropped red hair, she's as striking-looking a woman as I've ever seen, an observation Janine makes out loud even as I'm thinking the very same thing.

Reading the story, it's clear a life in the military was inevitable given her family's three-generation-long record of service. What's also clear is that she was destined not merely to join the military, but to lead, as she matter-of-factly says herself: "I was committed to being the best soldier imaginable and would accept no less than perfection from those under my command. Most of all, I would make certain that America always emerged victorious. Any opportunity to destroy the enemy would be taken. Any means of gaining the upper hand would be embraced. Any weapon, however brutal, would be deployed. Screw the niceties of battle. For me, life was war."

Charming. I can only imagine how her dating profile would read: Hobbies: playing tennis, going ballroom dancing, and mercilessly decimating enemy soldiers on the battlefield.

Janine and I fall silent after reading the article. If this woman is reporting directly to President Myra Winters and planning to do God knows what involving Louis and TimeLock, we may be facing an enemy who would make the late Patrick Loder seem like the Cowardly Lion by comparison.

"Google 'Carter Prescott,' will you?" Janine says. A few seconds later, her hunch is confirmed. "I knew it!" she exclaims as we see story after story featuring the Maryland-born Prescott and his good friend, Myra Katherine Winters.

"Sloane . . . Prescott. All roads lead back to Myra Winters," I say. "But what does it mean?"

"It means these are serious players and Yoshi has to get out of that police station right this minute. If Sloane finds out the cops are on the case, Louis and Kiyoko won't last a day."

I text Yoshi back. *Do NOT involve police. Say you made a mistake—everybody's fine. Then go to a safe location and call us.*

A few seconds later, Yoshi responds with a simple *Understood*, and I ask Janine, "So what now?"

"We pay a visit to your favorite stick-in-the-mud, Walter Greene."

Janine's boss and the least interesting man in the world.

"I'm bored already."

CHAPTER SIX

Walter Greene's home is as bland as Mr. FBI himself. It's not that he has bad taste, it's that he has no taste. Clearly, he's spent a good deal of money on this house, though, since Walter apparently inherited quite the tidy sum from his parents. None of that inheritance seems to have been spent on anything resembling stylish decor, but fortunately, we're not here from *House Beautiful*.

"I don't know what you want me to do with this," Walter tells us. Or, more accurately, tells Janine. "The president knows a lot of people and many of them are in the military. The connection to the alleged kidnapping is beyond tenuous."

"What's *alleged* is your skills as an agent," is what I'd love to say. Has he forgotten how right we turned out to be about Loder and Genescence? But, like a schoolmarm talking to a troublemaking student, Janine had told me before we got here to essentially stand in the corner and be quiet, so I comply.

"But you did look into Prescott for me, right?" Janine says.

"I did, and the man's a poster child for patriotism. Spotless record going back to childhood."

"This isn't out of thin air, Walter," Janine says with a decided edge—an edge the more cautious, respect-the-chain-of-command, pre-Morgan Janine would have been far less likely to display to her boss.

"We're convinced the president was involved with Loder and the cover-up," a feisty Janine continues. "Now, two years later, we have the inventor of TimeLock and his wife taken. We have a woman who's a trusted national security analyst for Myra Winters and a higher-up at Defense who's been a staunch supporter of the president for years. Meaning we have a trio of war hawks who think we're about to do the two-step with North Korea and may be willing to do everything they can to make sure America is the only one standing when the music stops. Doesn't all that strike you as just the slightest bit suspicious, Walter?"

"Not really. It's a small town. People cross paths all the time."

"And haven't you always said you don't believe in coincidences?"

"I believe in facts, Janine. And right now, all you two have, frankly, are wild conspiracy theories."

Realizing I'm not supposed to be privy to this particular FBI intel, Janine physically moves Walter to a corner of the room. Fortunately, despite my middle-aged hearing, I can pick up on almost everything she says: "Need I remind you what you told me about Bartlett's conversation with the future president a couple of years back? If she's still dead set on finding a way to weaponize TimeLock, this would be the perfect time and the perfect play. She thinks North Korea is about to storm the beaches of Malibu, so she enlists her gal pal Sloane Whalen and Prescott to force Garvey into service."

Walter thinks it over for a moment, then nods knowingly. He and Janine move back toward me, and Walter—much to our shock—says, "Listen, I was wrong last time. I don't want to make the same mistake again. I'll poke around and see what I can find out."

"Thanks, Walter," Janine says.

"Yeah, thanks Walter," I add, sincerely. Then residual guilt over relentlessly teasing Walter behind his back—especially given that his affidavit two years ago helped keep me out of jail and the fact that he'd been in love with Janine before I came along yet apparently holds no grudge—prompts me to tack on this random non-sequitur: "Nice house, by the way."

Janine looks over—*what?* But I think Walter appreciates the compliment.

"Tell you what," he says, suddenly my new best friend. "There's a local resident I've gotten very close to since his retirement who might have some insight into this matter."

Walter makes a call, and while we wait, Janine and I check out his tortuously boring glassed-in display case full of FBI pins, pens, and coins.

"Who needs TimeLock?" I joke. "If you want to punish criminals, just force them to look at this collection all day."

Janine laughs as Walter finally returns with a proud smile on his face and informs us he's gotten the green light for Janine and me to meet his neighbor. We know who it is because they've been friends for years, but we pretend to be clueless. All I know is that this particular friend had better help us, because if he doesn't, I may feel inclined to punch him in the face.

You guessed it, we're on our way to meet the man who authorized TimeLock and stole twenty years of my life from me: former president of the United States William T. Bartlett.

CHAPTER SEVEN

As I mentioned, I have all kinds of reasons to dislike William Bartlett; after all, TimeLock not only took a huge chunk out of my life, but cost Lonny and many others theirs. But we're here for information that might save our friends, so I promised Janine I'd leave my personal baggage out of this.

After exchanging greetings with Bartlett, we get to the subject at hand: President Myra Winters. And it doesn't take long to elicit a surprisingly candid response from the former chief executive.

"The buck stopped with me, so I take full responsibility for what went wrong with TimeLock," Bartlett says. "I had my doubts, but I let Myra steamroll her way into getting the program approved. And, for a while, it seemed to be working. Crime was being curtailed, and justice was being served."

I bite my tongue and let him continue. "If what you suspect is true, however, she knew it was all going south, then at least tacitly approved the cover-up by Loder. And may I say, the nation owes you both a debt of gratitude for bringing that cover-up to light."

"Thank you, Mister President," Janine says, and I manage a nod.

"Even though it took a toll on my approval numbers," he adds with a smile.

"Enough with the pleasantries!" I want to shout. Bartlett is covering familiar ground when we're desperate for new information. Walter told him about our theory that the president, Sloane Whalen, and possibly Carter Prescott may be behind the kidnappings in Japan, so all we really want to know is if he believes us and if he can help.

"Here's the thing and I say this with the greatest possible respect for the voting public and for the highest office in the land," Bartlett continues. "Myra Winters is certifiably bananas."

Now he's talking!

"You have to understand," adds Bartlett, "Myra is the worst kind of crazy. The kind that seems perfectly sane to the outside world. The kind who will do anything, however immoral or illegal it might be, to achieve their goals. The kind who truly believes they're doing the right thing."

"History is littered with human suffering courtesy of people who thought they were doing the right thing," Janine offers.

"Quite right," the former president says. "And, in fairness, Myra's objectives were noble—lowering crime, protecting the nation. But at what cost?" Bartlett shakes his head and continues, "I don't know what really happened between her and Patrick Loder. But I do know what went down in the Oval Office four years ago. And I think it might relate to the Department of Defense connection Walter mentioned."

Janine and I exchange glances. At last, Bartlett is moving this conversation in the right direction. And if he agrees with us that the president and her cronies are behind what's happening in Japan, the same man I've held in contempt since Lonny and I went through TimeLock might just turn out to be a formidable ally after all.

The former president now goes to his computer, presses some keys, then beckons us over. Janine and I move toward the monitor and find ourselves watching a confidential Senate Defense Committee hearing featuring the esteemed Dr. Lionel Garvey and dated about four years ago—shortly after he accidentally aged himself in the run-up to the program. Bartlett speeds the video forward, then stops as Garvey is pointing to a chart of the human body.

"Myra mentioned this hearing one day in the Oval. I think this is what gave her the idea."

He presses play and we hear Dr. Garvey say: "Putting aside the many moral reservations I have about the use of TimeLock on prisoners, we have to safeguard that the process isn't used by our enemies for nefarious purposes. More specifically, despite international laws prohibiting such an endeavor, I'm deeply concerned that TimeLock could be repurposed as a weapon of sorts. If dispersed in a gaseous form, a modified TimeLock formulation could cause an immediate genetic deterioration among our troops that would leave them highly vulnerable to injury, capture, or death."

Bartlett stops the video and we take our seats in his living room.

44

"Now, as rational people, I'm sure your reaction to that video was the same as mine—it sounds more than a little farfetched, not to mention illegal. But then again, much the same was said leading up to TimeLock, right? Anyway, when Myra came to the Oval to propose doing precisely what Doctor Garvey had warned us against, I told her point blank that such an idea was unthinkable and insane. Unfortunately, she had a very different take on it. For her, it was a given somebody would soon take the leap into biological warfare, so why shouldn't we be first?"

"And nothing would help her get to the finish line faster than forcing Doctor Garvey to oversee the project," Janine suggests.

Bartlett nods. "Quite so. His work is at least a decade ahead of everyone else's."

"And where would Brigadier General Prescott fit in?" I ask.

"He's as much of a hawk as the president is. My guess is he's helping siphon Defense funds for this operation."

"It does explain everything," Janine says.

Now I chime in again: "Okay, so it seems pretty clear. They knew Louis would never go along with any of this, so they grab his wife and give him no choice but to be a part of the madness."

"Unfortunately—it makes sense," President Bartlett says.

"The problem is," I say, "Doctor Garvey will never go along with it. He'll stall as long as he can, then sacrifice himself and hope they let his wife go free."

"Which of course they won't," says Janine.

"Meaning we have to find both of them before it's too late."

"I take it there's no proof of any of this, Mister President?" Janine asks. "No memos from Myra Winters to you when you were in office, no proposals or clandestine meetings with other witnesses."

"Nothing. But I'm not without my resources. I can contact the authorities in Japan. I can go on national television tonight and tell the world about my meeting with the current president four years ago. Anything to stop her in her tracks."

"Perhaps, sir, but for now I think we keep this under the radar," Janine responds. "If the president feels cornered, she'll get rid of the evidence, and that includes Doctor Garvey and Anna."

Janine now looks at me and resolutely says, "We have to go there immediately."

"Go *where* is the big question," I say. "We don't know where they are in Japan or even if they're still there at all."

"I doubt they were taken out of the country," says Janine. "Too risky."

"If they *are* still in Japan," Bartlett ventures, "they'd need a fairly remote facility to work in, because, as I understand it, kalopheen—the mineral that makes the TimeLock process possible—is highly unstable."

"Right," says Janine. "The last thing they'd want is another Chernobyl on their hands. And to minimize their risk, they want it to be as far away from potential tectonic activity as possible. Which is a tall order in Japan."

"They'd also want to keep the whole undertaking as stealth as they can," the former president says. "Meaning they're not going to build a whole new Genescence from scratch."

"They'd have to convert an existing facility," I say.

I gesture to the president—may I? He nods and I do some poking around on the computer as Janine and Bartlett talk. Ten minutes later I have a list of seven recently acquired facilities in Japan that might fit the bill. Three were already being used for medical research, with the other four being former textile and high-tech manufacturing plants that could easily be converted. Unfortunately, Sloane Whalen's name isn't attached to any of them like it was to the flower delivery van, but that just means we'll have to dig deeper.

We thank the former president, rush home, and pack our bags. Janine calls Walter to request a few days off for "family business" and he pretends to believe her. I put a few client meetings on hold, and then Janine and I head to a private airport where William Bartlett—calling in a few presidential favors—has a plane fueled up and ready to take us to Kyoto, Japan.

CHAPTER EIGHT

I'm living with a stunning girlfriend in a rather posh condo and flying on a private jet chartered by the former president of the United States. How's that for moving up in the world?

All that's on our minds, though, is rescuing our friends. If indeed we're up against not only Department of Defense big shots but the president herself, the odds of any of us making it out of this alive are laughable at best.

Which is why I keep asking Janine whether she should be calling in the cavalry, namely, her colleagues at the FBI or their Japanese counterparts. But she's convinced this would only spook Louis and Kiyoko's captors and quite possibly force them to do something rash, and I of course defer to her proven expertise. Not to mention two other rather salient facts: we have no idea where Louis and Kiyoko are being held (or if they're even together), and we're not sure who in our government we can trust.

We managed to catch a few fitful hours of sleep en route and have just landed at Kansai International Airport outside of Kyoto. We rent a car and hightail it to the Kyoto Hotel Okura where we've arranged to meet Yoshi at noon. We check in, clean up, and head back down to the lobby. We don't know what Yoshi looks like, but we doubt he'll have any trouble spotting two unkempt and utterly exhausted Americans in the crowd.

"Agent Price? Mister Eberly?" A sweet-faced young man approaches and bows. Yoshi is a bit short and a bit pudgy. He's also instantly likeable and even manages a warm smile despite the obvious emotional toll this whole situation must be taking on him.

We likewise bow, then introduce ourselves and move to a secluded corner. We fill him in as best we can and give him some good news we received on the plane right before landing: Walter and his team are working on tracking the white van and could have a lead for us at any time.

"How can I ever thank you for this?" Yoshi asks humbly.

"They mean the world to us," Janine says. "Now tell us everything you can."

"I was visiting from Osaka."

"That's where your farm is, right?" I ask, rather proud that I remember so much about Kiyoko's younger brother.

A puzzled look crosses Yoshi's face.

"Kiyoko mentioned that you're a farmer," I say.

Yoshi smiles. "Not a farmer. A pharmacist."

Janine shakes her head and smiles. "Way to go, Sherlock."

"Anyway," Yoshi continues, "Kiyoko and Louis had just returned the night before from their annual summer vacation in Shimodo, and I arrived at their home late afternoon Sunday. As I was parking, I saw two men forcing my sister into that van and they sped off. Moments later, a woman—I think—put Louis into a sedan and they drove off."

"Same direction?" Janine asks.

"No—different."

"And you've heard nothing from them or their kidnappers."

51

"Not a word."

"This woman," Janine says. "Very tall with short red hair?"

"Yes! Who is she?"

"We'll fill you in later," Janine responds, before delicately adding, "But just in case we've got this all wrong, I have to ask whether it's possible this has anything to do with your late father's . . . connections."

"You mean Yakuza. No, that was ten years ago. Some of the men I grew up with still have a connection to the organization and they promise me this was unrelated."

"Are you sure you can trust them?" I ask.

"I know it seems strange, but there is a code of honor among these men. I believe them. In fact, a few of my friends even offered to help me if they could."

Janine thinks it over. "We might just take them up on that." She looks at me and says, "Add a little unofficial muscle to our little ragtag group here."

I nod. Fine by me.

It's time to check in again with Walter. I'm about to fill Yoshi in on our prevailing Sloane Whalen/Myra Winters, new-and-improved TimeLock theory when Janine suddenly reaches into her bag and pulls out her gun. And now I see why—two Caucasian men, one with a pronounced limp, are hurrying toward us from another corner of the lobby. We can't make out their faces, but we can definitely ascertain their intentions, so Janine, Yoshi, and I rush off toward a rear entrance.

Janine gestures and Yoshi and I follow her to our rented car. I take the wheel and we speed off, grateful beyond words I spent a month in New Zealand a few years ago and got (sort of) used to driving on the right side of a car and the left side of the road.

"Shit!" Janine yells and I look in the rearview mirror. The two men are climbing into their car and roaring toward us.

"Turn left here!" yells Yoshi, the only one of us who knows the back streets of Kyoto.

I make a wild last-minute turn, but the guys behind us don't miss a beat and stay right on our tail. Suddenly, our side mirror is smashed to bits in a hail of gunfire. Understandably desperate to get away from the shooting gallery, cars all around us veer off in all directions.

"Get down!" Janine yells to the terrified Yoshi in the back seat.

I continue to swerve erratically through traffic, hoping to lose our pursuers, but it isn't happening—if anything, they're getting closer. And with Yoshi crouched as low as possible in the back seat, he's forced to resign as our navigator. I'm on my own now.

I spot a bridge and shoot toward it as more gunfire explodes around us. Janine tries firing back, but the crazy sudden turns make it impossible for her to find a target. And that's when it strikes me: given how incredibly dangerous it is for me to be speeding through an unfamiliar city—on the left side of the road, no less—it's increasingly possible that I'll kill us all in a car crash before our pursuers even catch up to us.

I manage to drive around a few cars and gain enough distance to prevent the men chasing us from firing any more shots. For the moment. During the lull, a brave Yoshi lifts his head high enough to see where we are.

"Shinano River," he says. "Turn left when you see a sign for Garden Blossom Road."

"Yoshi," I shout, "I can't read Japanese!"

"Sorry—look for a big yellow sign with a picture of a ski resort. Then left."

"Got it."

Just now, our car is hit again by gunfire. As before, I veer all over the place but our pursuers are almost directly behind us. What I wouldn't give to hear a police siren right now, but no such luck.

"There!" Janine shouts, pointing to the yellow sign. Instead of turning left, though, I drive right past it. "You missed the turn!" Janine screams.

"I don't think so," I say as I suddenly make a dangerously sharp right turn, soar through a gas station, then cross the road and speed up Garden Blossom Road. Poor Yoshi is screaming from his crouched position in the back seat, but Janine gives me a smile and a thumbs-up. We've lost our tail again, but I'm sure they'll be reuniting with us all too soon.

"This is my fault," I say.

"How is it your fault?" Janine asks as I drive as fast as possible up an increasingly steep mountain road.

"They must have traced it back to me when I hacked into the flower delivery company's records. Which means they've been tracking our moves ever since."

"That was inevitable, wasn't it? Think who we're dealing with here."

"So I see two possibilities," I say. "They kill us now, or we escape and they move Louis and Kiyoko to God knows where and we never find them."

"There's a third possibility." This said in a whisper from Yoshi, as if he's afraid of being overheard by the goons chasing us.

"We die, but we don't die. Like Paul Newman and Robert Redford."

Janine doesn't have a clue what he's talking about, but a moment later, I do. "Butch and Sundance jumping off the cliff!" I say.

"Exactly!" Yoshi says. I had to travel to the other side of the world and get shot at to find him, but I've finally found my very own pop culture doppelganger.

"What are you two talking about?"

"We kill ourselves before they do it for us," I say to an understandably alarmed Janine. "Get ready, gang, it's showtime!"

Right on cue, the sedan chasing us appears in my rearview mirror. I have to make this next piece convincing, so I start weaving the car around as we climb up the winding road toward the summit. Even Janine can't hold back a scream or two, but I don't let up—this has to be believable.

A minute later, we turn another curve and are out of our pursuer's line of sight. I slow the car down.

"Everybody out!"

Now Janine gets it. I turn the wheel toward the edge of the road as the three of us burst out of the car and scramble behind some trees. A moment later, the sedan approaches just in time to see our car fly off the side of the road and soar a thousand feet to a virtually inaccessible crevice below. Unlike in the movies, the car doesn't randomly burst into flames on its way down or even when it crashes, but nobody looking at the crumpled heap of metal below would think for a second that there were any survivors.

The two men in the sedan—just far enough from us that we can't make out their faces—get out and look over the edge, clearly satisfied with a job well done. They get back in the sedan, turn it around, and drive back toward Kyoto.

Yoshi, Janine, and I give each other relieved hugs, then Yoshi turns to me and says, "Thank you, Morgan. You saved our lives."

"Your idea, Yoshi."

"Let's call it teamwork. What matters is we're still alive!"

I squeeze his shoulder, smile, and say what any James Bond fan who just faked his own death would say, especially in Japan of all places.

"You only live twice."

CHAPTER NINE

It's been a day since Janine, Yoshi, and I plunged to our "deaths," and we've been laying low on the outskirts of Kyoto ever since. Fortunately, we've had help from a bunch of former Yakuza members who grew up with Kiyoko and her brother and who still feel a sense of loyalty to their late father.

I was expecting a bunch of ruffians but they're all highly educated and unfailingly polite. I'm certain these impressive young men will be essential to our plan— whenever we actually have one.

In addition to providing us with a place to stay, Yoshi's friends have volunteered to help us rescue Kiyoko and Louis when the time comes. And for that we will be eternally grateful, especially since we can't go to the police, can't formally involve the FBI, and, as mentioned, don't know who in the US government other than President Bartlett and Walter Greene we can possibly trust.

We do get some good news, however. Walter and his team have tapped into Jeiso Flowers' digital records and traced the elusive white delivery van to a home only twenty-five miles from here. Which means we could possibly have Kiyoko out of there by afternoon.

Or not, because when Janine, Yoshi, and I get to the address Walter sent us (driving a car borrowed from one of Yoshi's friends), there's no van in sight. And no home either. Instead, we find ourselves staring dejectedly at a vacant lot. We get out and walk around briefly just in case we're missing something, but it soon becomes clear that the flower company's owner was given fake info so nobody would be able to do precisely what we're trying to do.

"Damn it," Janine says.

"Now what?" I ask her.

"We find the owner of Jeiso Flowers and get some answers."

"How would he know where they took the van?"

"Most delivery companies have trackers on their vehicles. With any luck, he installed one and we can locate our missing van on his computer."

Just to momentarily relieve the tension, I turn to Janine and ask, "Just out of curiosity, why does everyone with a badge say *vehicle* instead of *car* or *truck*?"

Janine smiles and says, "Get your ass in the 'vehicle' and let's get the hell out of here."

"Yes, sir."

We then ask Yoshi to call the now defunct Jeiso Flowers and pretend he's interested in buying a couple of the vans. Fortunately, the company's owner, Akinari Tanaka, is there, so Yoshi, Janine, and I head to Jeiso's home office only a few miles away on the outskirts of Kyoto.

While I'm hardly in Kyoto to sightsee, the drive to Tanaka's office affords me a few minutes to take in my surroundings, something that's certainly easier to do in a car that isn't being pummeled by gunfire. Surrounded by mountains and brimming with life and culture, Kyoto is almost otherworldly in its majesty and I can't help but think how glorious it would be for me and Janine to someday experience Japan as normal tourists instead of as potential targets.

Twenty minutes later, we get out of the car and head toward Jeiso Flowers' main entrance. The door is locked so we ring a bell. No response. Just now, we react to the sound of a door opening on the side of the building. We run toward it in time to see a middle-aged man scurrying out and racing off behind the building. We all give chase, wondering what spooked this guy into bolting away from us.

In short order, both Yoshi and I—he a bit overweight and me a bit middle-aged—are winded, with only the annoyingly fit Janine gaining on what we assume must be Tanaka. Fortunately, he's no marathon runner himself, so it's only a matter of time before Janine just about catches up with him.

We get to a busy street and Tanaka runs inside a huge five-story department store. Not surprisingly, it's extremely crowded and therefore the perfect place for our runaway friend to blend in with the masses. But Janine spots him sprinting up the escalator, and Yoshi and I follow.

On the second floor, Tanaka runs toward a seemingly endless display of clocks and watches; an ironic setting because precisely a minute later, his time is up. Janine chases him into a corner, and a breathless Tanaka bows his head in defeat. An equally breathless Yoshi and I join them and Tanaka says something only Yoshi can understand in what sounds to me like a terrified and pleading voice.

Yoshi responds to him and Tanaka seems assuaged by what he's hearing. "He panicked when he saw the two of you," Yoshi says to me and Janine.

"Why?" I ask.

"Because you're Americans."

"I don't—"

"He thought we were part of Sloane Whalen's group, right?" Janine interjects.

"Exactly," says Yoshi. "Whatever they did, they scared him half to death. Especially the 'tall and terrifying woman with the short red hair' who he thought was going to kill him on the spot."

"Tell him I'm with the FBI and ask him if his vans have trackers."

Yoshi nods and talks to Tanaka in a calm and reassuring voice, but the older man remains frozen and silent.

"Tell him two lives and possibly many more are at stake," Janine urges. "And Yoshi, please assure him he'll be left out of it completely."

Exuding warmth and empathy in a manner that obviously comes naturally to him, Yoshi addresses Tanaka again, and finally the man nods reluctantly. A half hour later, we're huddled in front of Tanaka's computer and he calls up the van that was sold to Sloane. We get the van's current location—a home about fifteen minutes from here—thank a cautiously relieved Tanaka, and rush out the door.

Standing beside our car in front of Tanaka's building, we're all upbeat to have hopefully located Kiyoko, but a moment later Janine's expression suddenly changes. Clearly, she's troubled by whatever she's about to tell us.

"Obviously, we all want your sister freed as soon as possible," Janine says to Yoshi. "The question we have to answer is 'what then?'"

"I don't understand," he responds.

But now I realize what's on her mind, so I say this: "Yoshi, the only leverage these animals have over Louis is that they have his wife. If she goes free and he somehow finds out . . ."

"He stops working for them and he's instantly expendable, right?" Yoshi asks.

"Right," Janine answers. "Louis is probably stalling right now, but for the time being, they most likely don't know that."

It would have been completely understandable if Yoshi had exploded over the idea of keeping his sister a hostage a minute longer than necessary. But it's obvious he's far more mature and thoughtful at twenty-five than I would have been. If I had ever *been* twenty-five, that is.

"So, what do you have in mind?" Yoshi asks.

"That's where your pals come in." And Janine lays out a plan that's chock-full of risks, but does seem our best shot at rescuing Louis and Kiyoko both.

The plan goes something like this. First, we determine how many men are watching Kiyoko. Hopefully, it's still just the two goons who took her. Then, in the middle of the night, we introduce halothane into the home's ventilation system. This will render the guards unconscious for fifteen minutes or so. Most likely Kiyoko too, but we can wake her up once inside.

At this point, we give her a listening device that she'll of course keep hidden from her captors. Then we wait until the next time they have her call Louis—assuming, of course, that Sloane allows such conversations in order to keep Louis motivated.

"And during that call," Janine says, "she surreptitiously lets him know we're listening in and he tells us where he is. That is, if he even *knows* where he is."

Yoshi pauses a second, then asks the obvious question: "Won't the guards realize they were knocked out?"

"Doubt it," Janine tells us. "Middle of the night, they dozed off for a few minutes. Kiyoko is still there, sound asleep. No big deal. Status quo."

Showing the depth of his character yet again, our resident pharmacist Yoshi offers to help us acquire both the needed halothane and a stimulant to wake Kiyoko through his legit—and his friends' legit-ish—connections. And though we urge him to stay out of it to protect his career, it's obvious that protecting his beloved sister and brother-in-law is all he cares about right now.

"And if none of this works," Janine says, "There's always plan B. We go in guns blazing and bring your sister home safely."

CHAPTER TEN

I t's 3:30 a.m. and we've parked around the corner from the house where we assume Kiyoko is being held. The white flower delivery van is out front. Meanwhile, we're in two vans of our own—Janine, Yoshi, and me, along with three of Yoshi's friends in one, another four guys in the other.

Dressed in the requisite all black, the three men in our van get out and slink toward the back of the house. Minutes later, they return with good news: thanks to their sophisticated infrared surveillance equipment, they can confirm that Kiyoko is definitely inside and apparently unharmed, and that there are, thankfully, only two guards watching her.

The three men return to the house with their bag of goodies—four small canisters of halothane and a tiny listening device. Needless to say, they're fully armed in case this all goes south. And they're wired so their friends in the second van can swoop in if needed.

Trained FBI agent that she is, Janine was always going to go in once the guards were down. But she was absolutely against me, and especially Yoshi, joining her. Too many people, too many amateurs, and too much risk.

Yoshi and I reluctantly agreed, so we go to the second van where we can listen in on what's happening. Unfortunately for Janine, she fell in love with an impulsive and sometimes reckless man, so I leave a protesting Yoshi with his buddies and scramble off to catch up with Janine. Wearing an oversized black gas mask so as to avoid the effects of the halothane, I feel less like a super spy and more like I'm about to tell Luke Skywalker that I'm his father.

By the time I arrive at the back of the house, the three guys have already dispersed the sleeping agent inside. Naturally, Janine is furious to see me show up and I can see the anger on her face even though it's covered by a mask.

The three young men head inside and give us the thumbs-up. Both guards are in the living room, knocked out completely. Janine and I check out two bedrooms—nothing. But the third one's the charm—Kiyoko is asleep on the bed.

Janine shakes her, but as expected, the halothane has worked its magic on Kiyoko as well. And so Janine administers a shot, courtesy of Yoshi, and seconds later, Kiyoko's eyes shoot open.

"Janine! Morgan! Thank God . . ."

We give her big hugs and ask if she's being treated alright. She nods, then asks, "Do you have Louis?"

Janine shakes her head. "We don't know where he is. Do you?"

Kiyoko shakes her head as one of Yoshi's pals comes in and gestures—ten minutes until the halothane wears off. Janine fills Kiyoko in on the plan and she's fully on board with it. Kiyoko takes the listening device and hides it in her shirt.

"How often do they let you speak to him?" Janine asks.

"Every morning around ten. What is this all about? What do they want with us?"

"It's related to TimeLock. We can't explain now," Janine says. "Let's just pray he knows where they're keeping him."

I make a suggestion of what Kiyoko should say when she speaks to her husband, and we remind her our guys are just down the street listening in if they mistreat her or grow suspicious. We also tell her that Yoshi was integrally involved with our finding her but decide to lie and say he's safely standing by at a hotel. She has enough to worry about as it is.

Janine and I give Kiyoko a thumbs-up and head out of the house with our three knights in shining armor.

CHAPTER ELEVEN

The next morning at ten, Yoshi, Janine, and I are huddled in front of a receiver in the second van around the corner from where Kiyoko is being held. One of the guards in the house says, "Talk now" and we hear the following exchange between Kiyoko and her husband:

"Are they treating you well?" Louis asks.

"I'm alright. Please cooperate with them and we'll both be safe."

"I am. But if they so much as touch you—"

And here it comes. "I'll be fine, my love," Kiyoko says. "We've been through worse, right? Like when Janine and Morgan were listening in after they bugged the phone at our house and then told Loder we'd be hiding at the River Inn."

There's a pause and we hear a woman's formidably commanding voice coming from Louis's line. "You have thirty seconds." Sloane Whalen, no doubt.

If Louis picked up on the rather obvious clue, this is the moment we've been waiting for. He knows we never bugged his house and that it was Loder who tracked Janine and me to the River Inn. Hopefully, then, he realizes we're listening in to this call right now.

"For me," Louis finally says after an uncomfortably long silence, "the worst was the night Genescence burned down. With no less than the future president on hand as the one and only guest of honor."

"Enough reminiscing!" Sloane shouts.

"I love you," Kiyoko says in a whisper.

"I love you too," Louis responds, before quickly adding, "And when this is all over, we can finally take our usual seasonal vacation and forget this ever happened."

"This conversation is over," Sloane says, and the line is disconnected.

Janine, Yoshi, and I exchange looks.

"You think he picked up on it?" Janine asks.

"I think so," I respond. "That long pause—I bet he was scrambling to figure out exactly what to say without anyone but us catching on."

"Except we *didn't* catch on," says Janine.

"Not yet," I tell her. "Let's go over it word by word. First of all, what was all that about the night Genescence burned down? Why bring that up of all things?"

"There's something else," says Yoshi. "'Finally take our usual seasonal vacation'? They just got *back* from a seasonal vacation."

"That's right!" I say. "So he definitely wanted to draw our attention to that. But why?"

"Maybe they took him to the same place. Where did they go again?" Janine asks.

"Shimodo. They go there every summer."

"What's it like there?"

"Port town. Beaches. Hot springs. Very popular resort. You think that's where they're holding him?"

"Not on the list and seems unlikely that they'd pick a tourist destination, but maybe," I say. From Yoshi's puzzled look, I tell him about the list I put together at President Bartlett's house of the most likely facilities where they could be holding Louis.

"Okay, let's go over it again," I continue. "Louis mentions that night at Genescence, but why? And he draws our attention to their seasonal vacation. Another 'why?'"

Now Janine chimes in: "Let's start with Genescence. What did he say exactly?"

"The future president was there as a guest of honor," says Yoshi.

"Which we already knew since Janine and I were there that night," I say dejectedly.

"Hold on a second!" Janine says excitedly. "He didn't say she was '*a*' guest of honor, he said she was the '*one and only*' guest of honor."

"I don't understand," Yoshi says, but I do.

"Except she *wasn't* the only guest of honor," I venture with equal excitement. "She wasn't even the main guest of honor. The actual president of the United States was there and obviously . . ."

Janine finishes my sentence, "*He* was the star attraction."

"Meaning Louis was definitely trying to direct our attention to Myra," I say.

"He must know she's behind the whole thing," Janine continues. Then her face sags. "Problem is, while that may be news to him, we already know that. And that still doesn't explain the 'seasonal vacation' reference."

"Clearly, he wanted us to draw a straight line between the president and where he and Kiyoko take their annual vacation," I venture. "But what's the connection?"

As the minutes tick past, my frustration grows exponentially, and I feel like I'm trapped in an impenetrable escape room situated right inside my mind. I'm sure Janine and Yoshi feel the same way and are thinking the same thing: we may be forced to wait a full day before we can try this longshot gambit again. Only, Louis and Kiyoko may not have a full day if Sloane realizes he's only stalling. So I again run the sequence of words through my head over and over again. But I still can't break through and all I can think is, *What in God's name does the current president have to do with Louis and Kiyoko's annual summer vacation?*

And suddenly, milliseconds after thinking the word *name*, the answer hits me like a thunderbolt.

"My God!" I shout. It all makes sense now.

"What?" Janine and Yoshi both say in unison.

"Think about it. Louis said two seemingly unrelated things that both struck us as odd. The future president as the sole guest of honor when in fact she wasn't. And taking a 'seasonal' vacation when in fact they just took one. Of course—the man is brilliant!"

"Of course *what*, Morgan?" Yoshi says.

"Winters! The president's last name is Winters. He wasn't talking about her. He was talking about the time of year! We know they spend their summers in Shimodo. Yoshi, where do they spend their winters?"

"That's easy," he answers. "Hakone."

I pull out my phone, check the list I made at Bartlett's. There it is—number four: Hakone! "Secluded mountain town. Former headquarters of Nikea Medical Devices. Recently acquired by unknown buyer in America. Guys, I think we just found Louis."

"You know when I called you a reckless idiot last night when you followed me into the house?" Janine asks with a smile.

"Yeah?"

"You're still a reckless idiot. But you're also a friggin' genius!"

"That's what I've been trying to tell you the past two years," I say with a smile.

"So now we can call in the police, right?" a hopeful Yoshi asks.

"I'm afraid not, Yoshi," answers Janine. "We can't risk Whalen and Prescott getting wind of our plans. We'll have to go in alone."

A worried expression crosses Yoshi's cherubic face and he says, "*Watashitachi wa mechakuchadesu.*"

Trying to be as respectful as possible, I say, "That's lovely, Yoshi. What does it mean?"

Yoshi looks at me with a half smile and says, "We're screwed."

CHAPTER TWELVE

We're in one of the vans making the four-and-a-half-hour drive from Kyoto to Hakone. Three of Yoshi's friends stayed behind and will move in to extract Kiyoko as soon as we give the word. The four others, Akitoshi, Hiroki, Chikao, and Hikaro, are with me, Janine, and Yoshi. Although we have Yoshi on hand as a translator, I'm fine keeping the 'conversation' with these four gentlemen to a few grunts and groans—nobody is in the mood for small talk and we have no idea what we'll be up against once we arrive.

Risky though it is, we've decided to stage our raid during the daytime when Louis is most likely to be on the premises. Obviously, it would be easier to go in at night, but if they're housing him off-site, we'd have tipped our hand for nothing.

We reach Hakone around noon and understand immediately why Louis and Kiyoko have made this their wintertime getaway destination. It's picture-post-card stunning—a mountain town in Fuji-Hakone-Izu National Park west of Tokyo overlooking a lake and featuring spectacular views of Mount Fuji.

An hour later, we've parked our van behind some trees, and the six of us slink up the hill toward the high-tech complex that might as well be called Genescence East.

Yoshi reluctantly agreed to stay in the van again. The last thing we want is for him to get hurt or worse. Naturally, Janine wanted me to remain behind as well, but she knew that was never going to happen. Plus, given how many bad guys we may be up against, our little group needs all the help it can get.

Though I was forced to kill Patrick Loder's security chief/assassin-for-hire Neil Colby back at Genescence two years ago, I'm more than reluctant to fire the AR15 semi-automatic I'm carrying now. And not just for moral reasons; I've only had a couple of brief lessons from Janine in operating the damn thing.

Ironically, our four Yakuza colleagues were no less reluctant to be armed for this mission themselves since gun laws are so strict in Japan, even many criminals shy away from them. But given our limited resources and equally limited window of opportunity, they ultimately agreed and now we can only hope we'll be able to corner Sloane and her team before any shots are fired.

We split into groups of two and fan out. The place is immense, but Walter's people were kind enough to provide us with satellite images of the complex, along with schematics of the interior. Our first and, hopefully, only target is the main laboratory in the middle of the structure. This is where we expect to find Louis—at gunpoint, no doubt—doing his research and conducting his tests.

We get word via walkie-talkie from Hiroki and Chikao—they're at the periphery of the lab. Yoshi translates for us: inside, his friends have spotted eight or nine men and one very tall woman with striking short red hair—Sloane Whalen, of course, a stand-out figure most anywhere but especially here in Japan where she towers above just about every man and woman alike.

Janine and I head toward the vast lab from a different angle, as do Akitoshi and Hikaro. Just when I'm thinking getting this far inside has been too easy, though, an alarm starts blaring and machine guns start blazing in all directions. Hiroki and Chikao are the first to be spotted by the guards, and they're the first to go down in a hail of bullets.

The rest of us spread out and fire back, taking out two of the guards. We now see Sloane race toward a corner of the lab and pull someone away with her—it's Louis! They exit the laboratory and are out of sight. I gesture to Janine and we run in that direction, radioing Akitoshi and Hikaro that our target has been taken into another section of the building.

As they race along the outer rim of the lab to join up with us, both men are suddenly gunned down and the shooter looks our way and fires. Bullets go flying all around us, and now the man, the same one with the limp who pursued us when we arrived in Kyoto, moves as quickly as he can in our direction. He's joined by two other guards, but Janine is able to wound one of them in the leg.

Janine and I make it to the rear of the lab and find ourselves in a cavernous manufacturing facility, clearly once used to produce huge quantities of medical equipment. Where once this room must have been deafeningly loud during production hours, there's now an eerie silence pervading the space—a silence only interrupted by the sporadic firing of guns from both ahead of and behind us.

Janine gestures—we have to split up. I seem to recall her once using the phrase "clustering the target," and having us both side by side makes us far too vulnerable. So, I reverse course and hide behind some machinery as Janine presses ahead to wherever Sloane might have taken Louis. A few seconds later, a barrage of bullets hits the equipment all around me. I peek out but nobody is there. The shooter must have moved on, so I gingerly step out, only to hear a vaguely familiar voice.

Hello, Morgan," a man says. "Drop it." I put my gun down and turn around to find myself staring into the face of the man with the limp. And it's a face I know all too well.

"Hello, Neil," I say to Neil Colby, Patrick Loder's murderous second-in-command and the man who actually murdered Lonny Myers two years ago.

"What brings you to Japan this time of year, Neil?" I ask in a forced casual voice that barely conceals my shock at seeing Colby alive again. "Just killing time, or just killing?"

"You and your girlfriend are still trying to save the world, I see," a smirking Colby says.

"As long as you keep screwing it up."

"I've been looking forward to ending you both for two years. I hope you'll make it worth the wait."

He lifts his rifle and is about to shoot when three rapid-fire shots smash into the equipment near where Colby is standing. I'm not even sure where they came from, but I take advantage of the momentary distraction and dive toward him. I crash into him and kick his gun away, lift mine and get ready to fire. But even a weakened Colby is five times stronger than I'll ever be, so we grapple on the floor for a few seconds until he's got a hold of my gun. Game over.

Colby smiles victoriously. But just then, a single shot rings out, and this one hits him right in the heart. A stunned Colby drops back to the ground, and I look over to see my rescuer emerge from a corner of the room.

It's Yoshi. He's shaking but manages a proud smile. I squeeze his shoulder in gratitude and we run toward Janine.

CHAPTER THIRTEEN

A few moments later, we hurry into a large office and are shocked to see Janine standing unarmed and helpless. And then we see why—Sloane is holding a gun to Louis's head. She gestures, and Yoshi and I are forced to drop our weapons as well.

"Patrick Loder told me you two were a real pain in the ass," Sloane says.

"Let him go," I say.

Sloane smiles—yeah, sure. "No, I think what I'll do is kill all of you," she says before looking at Louis and adding, "then make a call and take care of your wife."

"And how do you think that will go down with your boss in the White House?" Janine asks. "No Garvey, no program."

Sloane smiles. "He was never going to deliver. We'll just have to find someone else who's a bit more . . . with the program."

"You do realize the 'program' is madness, don't you?" I say.

"No. Madness is waging war without every possible advantage. The good doctor here could help us weaken our enemies right there on the battlefield, but instead he hides behind a veil of moral righteousness. Because he's never been on a battlefield, I'm guessing. He's never watched his brothers and sisters and buddies get blown to pieces by adversaries whose only morality is to kill as many American soldiers as they possibly can. Don't you love your country, Eberly?"

"The end justifies the means, right?" I say. "Only problem with that is where does it stop? We turn to genetic engineering on the battlefield, our enemies turn to chemical warfare. We turn to cellular degeneration, they turn to nuclear annihilation."

"No, they turn back and surrender," Sloane retorts. "Because they know the reality is they can never defeat us."

"And what if they don't accept reality," Janine says. "What if they live in a fantasy world like you and Prescott and Myra Winters?"

"I would think you of all people would understand what we're trying to do here, Agent Price."

"What is that supposed to mean?" Janine asks.

"It means you've sworn allegiance to your country the same as I have. It means you believe in law and order the way I do. I would have thought it also means you would do anything and everything you can to make sure the sanctity of our democracy is never threatened."

"And what if the threat is coming from within?" says Janine. "What if the threat is coming from *you*?"

"I don't follow," Sloane says.

"Don't you think launching a new era of chemical warfare could do more damage to the 'sanctity of our democracy' around the world than any foreign power ever could? Don't you think what you're doing here would so damage America's global moral standing—one that's already taken quite a few body blows over the past twenty-five years—that we might never recapture it again?"

"Time will tell, Agent Price. Time will tell."

Janine smiles at Sloane and says, "I'm afraid you're all out of time, dear."

She suddenly pulls out a gun hidden above her ankle and fires a shot that hits Sloane in her right shoulder. Warrior that she is, Sloane manages to get off a shot in

Janine's direction, but thankfully it misses. As Janine prepares to fire back, Sloane manages to escape through a side door.

As she does, we rush forward and embrace the trembling Louis, then Janine contacts the three men outside of the house where Kiyoko is being held and shouts, "Go! Go! Go!"

Minutes later, Janine tells Louis that his wife is safe, and though we took heavy losses, our operation has been a success.

And in a touching reminder how he puts Kiyoko's safety far above his own, a deeply relieved Louis quietly says, "Thank you for saving my wife."

CHAPTER FOURTEEN

A few minutes later, Janine, Louis, Yoshi, and I race outside the building in time to see Sloane getting into a car. Even with the bullet wound to her shoulder, she still manages to maneuver a fairly large steel container onto the passenger seat.

"The kalopheen vials!" a distressed Louis yells. "I think she has the entire supply. If we don't recover it, they'll just set up shop somewhere else and we're back to square one."

Reacting to Yoshi's understandably confused look, I tell him, "It's the secret sauce behind TimeLock."

I turn toward Yoshi and say, "You still have the gun, right? In case anyone's still here."

Yoshi pats his jacket and nods, after which I gesture for him and Louis to stay put while Janine and I rush toward our van. Deferring to Janine's FBI training and typical take-charge demeanor, she gets behind the wheel, I climb into the passenger seat, and we roar off in pursuit of Sloane Whalen.

Minutes later, we find ourselves speeding behind Sloane's car on the famous (and treacherous) Hakone Turnpike Pass—a road that looks like it was sliced out of the mountain by some gigantic runaway drafting compass. Think San Francisco's Lombard Street from *Bullitt* on steroids.

With every foot we climb and every corner we turn, our fear grows more pronounced—not just the fear of meeting our demise on this terrifyingly twisty spaghetti strand of a road, but of letting Sloane and her precious cargo get away. And at the speed Sloane is driving, it's quite possible we'll never catch up to her.

But then something bizarre happens. Sloane's car pulls over and comes to a stop. We cautiously brake a few yards behind her, certain she's lured us here so she can easily mow us down. But that's not what happens at all. Sloane emerges from her car and holds her hands up in surrender. Janine and I exchange wary looks—*surrender* and *Sloane Whalen* simply don't belong in the same sentence. Something is very wrong here.

And then we understand. Sloane's injury was much worse than we thought. She knows she's going fast and has decided to make this her final stand. She gives us a triumphant smile before crumpling to the pavement.

Janine and I run over. Knowing she's taking her last breaths, Sloane looks up at us and says in a surprisingly strong voice considering her injuries: "I'm not the enemy. I never was. Complacency is the enemy. Tell Myra I'm sorry I won't be here to see it, but that the mission will live on without me."

Sloane manages a slight self-satisfied chuckle and then her eyes close. Janine checks her pulse to confirm that she's dead. I reach into the passenger seat and take out the steel container. We open it and now realize why she felt she felt she deserved the last laugh—the container is empty.

"Damn it!" Janine shouts. "This was nothing but a wild goose chase!"

We try to reach Louis and Yoshi on our cells, but no luck. Surmising the kalopheen must still be back at the lab, we get in the van and rush back. Normally, the FBI agent in Janine would wait for the police to show up so we could explain what happened to Sloane, but this is hardly a sanctioned operation to begin with, so the sooner we get out of here, the better.

CHAPTER FIFTEEN

F ifteen minutes later, we're back at the lab, but Louis and Yoshi aren't there. Damn it—even armed, they never should have been left alone. I run through the possibilities in my mind—one of Sloane's surviving henchman could have taken them, or maybe it was Carter Prescott himself. Which means that we've saved Kiyoko but Louis will be forced to cooperate or be eliminated on the spot. And I don't even want to imagine what they'll do to Yoshi.

Janine and I enter the facility and look around, praying that we've got this all wrong. Ten minutes later, we're on the lower level of the facility and ready to give up the search when we see Louis and Yoshi getting off an elevator, waving and heading our way. Janine and I hurry toward them and give them both big hugs that they appreciate but don't quite understand.

"We thought they took you—or worse," I tell Louis and Yoshi.

"Sorry about that," says Louis. "I wanted to double check to make sure she didn't leave any of the kalopheen supply in the storage room."

He shakes his head and adds, "All gone, I'm afraid."

"What happened with Sloane?" Yoshi asks. "She get away?"

"In a matter of speaking," Janine responds. "She's dead."

To which I add, "That's the good news. The bad news is she was a decoy. She didn't take the compound with her after all. Someone else did."

"Which means it's hopeless," says Louis.

"Afraid so," I tell him. "But they don't have you, so that should buy us precious time."

"I wouldn't be too—" Louis's words are suddenly cut off by the sound of a large explosion emanating from the north side of the facility. Seconds later, a second explosion rocks the southern section of the building, a section much closer to where we're standing. Ceilings and walls begin to crumble, and we race toward the stairwell to avoid the decimation.

"Did your team plant explosives?" Louis asks.

"No, of course not," Janine answers. "This must be part of Sloane's contingency plan. The building's in self-destruct mode."

"Oh, swell," I say before unnecessarily adding, "Let's get out of here!"

Just then, the level above us is shaken by a series of new explosions, and we all exchange frightened glances. The entire structure could be blown to pieces within minutes.

Yoshi then asks the obvious question, "How about going down?" As if the building has somehow heard him, though, it delivers its answer loud and clear when the floor below us is suddenly blown to pieces.

"Or not," Yoshi says.

"There's no way out," I say.

"Then we stay in," Louis replies enigmatically. "Follow me!"

Running behind Louis, we rush toward a door in the corner of the large room we're in and then down a flight of stairs in back of a small lunchroom. As the building continues to erupt in flames, smoke, and debris all around us, we find ourselves led by Louis into what looks like a newly constructed steel vault that's amazingly untouched by destruction.

Louis closes the thick vault door and we take in our surroundings—a freezing-cold storage room dotted with vacant shelves and empty metal containers. A minute ago, we were all scrambling for our lives in a crumbling building; now we're Burgess Meredith in "The Twilight Zone," sheltered in a bomb-proof vault that's our only protection from the apocalypse.

Louis says, "This is where the kalopheen was stored. If they fortified it correctly, this room is impenetrable. We should be safe until the self-destruct sequence is over."

Louis then produces a small smile and adds, "Unless we freeze to death first, of course."

After shivering our way through the next fifteen minutes, we realize the explosions have finally stopped. We cautiously exit the vault and perilously make our way up and out of what's left of the building.

As expected, we hear the sound of sirens speeding our way. If we weren't in such a remote mountainous location, I'm sure they would have been here already, but we're glad they're not. This gives us time to climb in our van and get the hell out of here. Formal explanations to the authorities will have to wait. Right now, we need to find the missing kalopheen compound and stop President Myra Winters in her tracks.

Driving away, Yoshi is looking back at the smoldering remains of the facility. I squeeze his shoulder. "I'm so sorry about your friends," I say. Yoshi nods. "They were brave and died with honor."

Yoshi radios the team in Kyoto and learns that they've already taken Kiyoko to a secure location in the city. Janine and I exchange glances, relieved beyond words that our friends are safe, but wondering if Sloane Whalen was right and the mission is already continuing on without her.

CHAPTER SIXTEEN

48 HOURS LATER

Okay, we were wrong about him. Sort of. Yes, former President William Bartlett has earned his milquetoast reputation now and then—most especially when he let Myra Winters steamroll him into approving the original TimeLock project despite his considerable reservations.

But he came through for us when we visited him at his home, and what he's doing right now is decidedly the opposite of wimpy. With Walter's help, Bartlett has returned to the bridge of the Enterprise—the Oval Office itself—and he's wired for sound via a tiny 007-worthy transmitter even White House security couldn't detect.

Given the roles Janine and I are about to play in this semi-legal but risky "entrapment," we're listening in from Louis and Kiyoko's home in Kyoto.

"You almost pulled it off," Bartlett says to President Winters.

"What are you talking about, Bill?" the president says.

"Garvey. His wife. Your little hit squad. Your insane genetics program."

"I have no idea—"

"Don't insult my intelligence, Myra. You had the man's wife kidnapped so you could unleash a deadly new era of genetic warfare on the world. It was nuts four years ago when you first broached the idea to me, and it's nuts now."

"You see, there's your problem right there, Bill," says the president. "You always thought small. You have the North Koreans itching to start a nuclear war and you do nothing. You have enemy combatants massing all over the Middle East and you do nothing. You're Neville Chamberlain without the British accent."

"Perhaps, but I never broke the law. You oversaw a massive cover-up when TimeLock was first launched, and God knows how many innocent people died because of that."

"Innocent? They were prisoners, remember? Murderers and thieves nobody in the world will ever miss."

"And what about Anna Garvey? More collateral damage?"

"You want me to apologize for putting my country first? Sorry—not going to happen. But you'll never understand because you can't think beyond playing by the book, toeing the line, staying the course. You know something, the history of this nation has been defined by three distinct types of presidents—the bold, visionary risk-takers like me; the corrupt power grabbers; and then, the worst kind of all, the kind of president you were, the mediocrities. The ones who not only couldn't push the envelope, but couldn't even find it in the first place. The ones who couldn't do anything unexpected if their lives depended on it. Didn't you ever wonder why they made this office oval, Bill? So that squares like you would never fit in here."

"How's this for unexpected, Myra? Your very own comrade in arms Sloane Whalen is prepared to testify about everything she did at your personal behest. In fact, she's leaving Japan for DC in three hours."

"Impossible. Sloane's dead."

"Your intel got it wrong. She escaped. I have my sources too, you know. And I assure you she isn't taking the fall for you."

"This is bullshit. Nobody's been able to reach her for two days."

"Keep trying."

Bartlett leaves and we lose our sound with his departure. But if our prediction is correct, the phone Janine is holding—the very same phone the Hakone police turned over to her after finding it in Sloane's getaway car on the Turnpike—will be ringing any second.

Sure enough, after a tense couple of minutes, the secure FaceTime call comes in.

"Madame President!" "Sloane" answers, her live feed beaming directly into the Oval Office.

"Where the hell have you been? I thought you were dead!" The president looks like she's about to explode with anger.

"Almost, but I got out."

"What have you told them? The FBI or whoever you're dealing with?"

"The truth, Madame President. That you ordered me to hold Anna Garvey hostage and force her husband to repurpose TimeLock into a chemical weapon for potential military use. And that I was to eliminate both of them when the job was finished."

"So instead of following my orders, your whole operation is brought down after a few short days by a bunch of amateurs, the program is delayed and maybe even compromised forever, and on top of that, you let Garvey and his wife get away. This was all your doing, Sloane!"

"And this will all be your undoing, Madame President."

The president's demeanor changes. Looking almost hurt, she says, "How could you do this to me?"

"I had no choice."

"Of course you had a choice! Your orders were clear. No connection to me under any circumstance. Why the fuck do you think I trusted you to handle this in the first place? Because I was relying on your professionalism and your discretion. On your . . . friendship. Then you fail me on all three counts? Think again, Sloane. Turn on me and you won't live another twenty-four hours!"

"Oh, but I have to live another twenty-four hours," "Sloane" says. "Because I want to be around this time tomorrow when you and your sorry administration become history."

"What?" the president shouts. And then her face turns ashen white as she watches the image of Sloane Whalen she's been seeing fade from view, only to be replaced by the face and voice of FBI Special Agent Janine Price.

"Afraid your pal Sloane didn't make it after all," Janine says.

Myra Winters can barely speak and the image grows shaky as the soon-to-be-former president tremulously begins to grasp what's happening to her. "I don't understand . . ."

"Seems I have a boyfriend who can work wonders with FaceTime and deep fake video," a smiling Janine responds. "Say hi, Morgan!"

I squeeze next to Janine, and I'm more than ready for my close-up.

"Hi there, Madame President," I say in a sing-song voice. "What with your imminent resignation and all, this probably isn't the best time to tell you, but I didn't vote for you. Sorry."

The president drops her phone to the ground. All we can see is the base of the Resolute Desk, and all we can hear is the sound of Myra Winters sobbing in disbelief.

Thanks to Walter, President Bartlett, Janine, and me, two hours later the handcuffed and disgraced president will trade the White House for the big house and will never be in a position of power ever again.

CHAPTER SEVENTEEN

Back home from Japan a week later, I wake up to find an email in my inbox from an address I don't recognize. Curious, I open it and start reading and find my eyes welling with gratitude as I do so. I beckon Janine over and she sits next to me and leans in to read the message:

Dear Morgan,

I'll be sending a similar message to Agent Price, but I wanted to thank you for your patriotism, for your bravery, and for your determination against untold odds to expose the world to the truth about TimeLock and about Myra Winters (call me petty, but I refuse to affix the title of President to her name).

Rather than letting bitterness toward TimeLock define your life, you put yourself in peril time and time again over the past two-plus years to do what was right for the country and for the world. In the process, you made certain one president would admit the error of his ways and that his successor would be brought down by the error of hers.

I see now that TimeLock in and of itself was, ironically, the greatest crime of all. But I hope you can take comfort in knowing that for all the years you have left—and thank goodness there will still be many—you will be considered a true national hero.

God bless you, and God bless the United States of America.

Sincerely yours,

William Bartlett

Janine and I exchange looks and she squeezes my shoulder in pride. Neither of us says a word because there are no words that could equal the ones we've just read.

In reality, neither Janine nor I will ever be considered national heroes for our role in derailing the Myra Winters crazy train because we have no intention of making that role public. First of all, Janine's FBI career in part depends on complete anonymity, and, second of all, I have no desire to spend the rest of my life fearing retribution from the disgraced former president's still-loyal followers.

Fortunately, though, this deeply moving tribute from President Bartlett, a man I once despised but have come to respect, is all the recognition we need. Which is precisely what I tell the former president in the heartfelt thank-you message I send a few minutes later.

A half hour after that Janine receives a similarly glowing email from President Bartlett and likewise thanks him for his kind words. Look at us—hobnobbing with a former president and responsible for the ascension of the newest one, Joseph Ayres, an eminently likeable and highly respected figure who's committed to bringing the nation together after Myra Winters did her best—or is that her worst?—to tear it apart.

That evening, Janine and I sit down on the patio and pour a couple of chardonnays. Like me, she's comfortable with silence, content to let what remains unsaid speak volumes. And though we don't say it out loud, I'm sure she's thinking what I am—it's a miracle how far we've come since that fateful day when she first arrested me. A day when, in her mind, I was just some punk kid capable of murder, and in mine, she was just some stiff-suited automaton incapable of emotion. How wrong we both were, and how right it feels that we've somehow wound up together.

Unless I decide to write a book about it one day, only a handful of people will ever know what Janine and I have been through since all this started, but like I said, we're good with that. Of course, we're not good with the fact that Sloane Whalen's mentor and former Defense Department superior Carter Prescott is still out there or that we let the precious supply of kalopheen be taken from the Hakone lab. But for now, we have the best reward of all—each other. And while our nightmare with TimeLock has hopefully ended, our dream of being together forever is definitely only just beginning.

CHAPTER EIGHTEEN

I 'm not sure which was more embarrassing, shopping for my girlfriend's engagement ring with my mother three months after Janine and I got back from Japan, or the sales clerk assuming the ring was *for* my mother since we're both in our mid-forties now. In any case, knowing Janine's taste leans on the less-is-more, nothing-too-flashy side, I managed to select an elegant ring I think she'll like.

Best of all, it's amazing how right this all feels. I laugh to myself now and then when I realize I practically spent more time in the capsule going through TimeLock than I spent with some of the girls I dated before meeting Janine.

But they weren't Janine, of course. They weren't the one who put her career and her life on the line over and over again to help some twenty-three-year-old-turned-forty-three-year-old stranger who fancied himself Easy Rider. A kid who in reality was just a high-strung loner with a lot of brains but not a lot of smarts.

I've said this before, but there's a small part of me that's grateful for what TimeLock did to me. Not for the precious years it took from me, of course, but for helping me evolve beyond the recklessness of youth and become the best person I could possibly be.

After being processed through TimeLock, I appeared middle aged but still felt like I was in my early twenties. Now, thanks to all this time in a committed relationship and my close friendships with Louis, Kiyoko, and now Yoshi—not to mention helping bring down a deadly prison program and an even deadlier megalomaniacal president—I feel like the forty-five-year-old I am.

You might say I've grown into the part.

That night, I bring home flowers and candy, open a bottle of wine, and get down on one knee. It's exactly two years to the day since Janine first arrested me, I remind her, and she breaks into a wonderful mix of laughter and tears.

"Will you marry me?" I ask.

"How can you ask such a silly question?" she says and my heart sinks. Then she smiles and adds: "How can you ask such a silly question when you already know the answer? Yes, a thousand times, yes!"

We kiss, then kiss again, then forget all about the wine and candy.

Five weeks later, we have only a month to go before our wedding at the Potomac Club, which would normally be way out of our price range if it weren't for Walter Greene pulling a few strings with management. Naturally, he'll be among the guests. Plus one, of course. Assuming, that is, he can find a mannequin who's free that night.

Okay, okay. After all he's done for us, I promise never to tell another dumb Walter-Greene-is-dull joke again in my life. In fact—and this is just between us—the surprising truth is that I've actually grown rather fond of the man.

Naturally, my mother and some of our relatives will be at the wedding, as will Janine's family. And speaking of my mother, I would love for her to start a life with someone new just as I have, but apparently there's nobody she's interested in right now. The reality is, I actually wish she'd remarry at this point—strange as it would be for a man my mother's age to suddenly have a stepson who's *also* my mother's age! Now how's that for a future sitcom premise? But for now, my mother seems content to remain on her own, so I leave well enough alone. Maybe I'll find someone for her one day, but if she's in no rush, I guess I shouldn't be either.

As a reflection of my newfound maturity, I've also even invited my two on-and-off friends Ben and Eric from my QuickRight Financial Services days. They wanted nothing to do with me when I was on the run after escaping from prison two years ago, and I won't deny that it hurt at the time. But I soon realized I had put them in an untenable position, so any hard feelings I held toward them have long since dissipated.

Best of all, Louis, Kiyoko, and Yoshi will not only be on hand for the wedding next month (with Louis as my best man and Kiyoko as matron of honor), but they've actually been in town for a couple of weeks now.

Ever considerate of others, even potential competitors, Louis has been helping a fellow geneticist named Dr. Emory Layton set up his own research lab using some of the same equipment that was misused during the Genescence days. Named GenQuest Bio-Tech Research, the new company is following Louis's example and seeking genetically based treatments to help forestall the ravages of aging. Much the same kind of work Louis has continued doing back in Japan.

And while we're on the subject of Japan, Janine and I have decided that's where we want to go on our honeymoon. Other than the constant danger (and the tragic loss of four of Yoshi's brave young friends), we fell in love with both the country as a whole and Hakone in particular. And it's safe to say Hakone will be a tad more enjoyable without Neil Colby and Sloane Whalen shooting at us.

Two other bits of news since Louis, Kiyoko, and Yoshi arrived and the first one just went down yesterday When Yoshi agreed to take a research job at GenQuest Bio-Tech Research. Apparently, he made a very positive impression on Dr. Layton when Louis introduced them (as he makes a positive impression on everyone), and he's agreed to relocate to DC by year's end.

I feel bad for Kiyoko and Louis, but we've promised to take very good care of our lovable young friend. In fact, Janine is already playing matchmaker and has seated one of her younger female colleagues next to Yoshi at our reception in the hopes that sparks will fly.

Then came the biggest news of all, and the real reason Louis wanted to be with us a month out from the wedding. He and I are on the porch at the condo, the others just inside.

"I may have a rather unique wedding present for you," he tells me. "Actually, it's for me as well. Have I ever mentioned the St. Augustine Project?" Louis asks.

"I don't think so."

"Before I was taken to Hakone—and I still can't believe you figured out where I was, by the way—I was working on something in my free time. Call it an obsession of mine, if you will."

"St. Augustine as in the Fountain of Youth?"

"The very same."

"My God—rejuvenation. Your life's dream."

Louis smiles.

"Louis, are you telling me you found it, an actual fountain of youth?"

"Well, not in the way you think. I can't turn the clock back for just anyone." He pauses for a moment and a broad smile crosses his face. "But I might be able to for us."

"You mean . . ."

"I mean anyone who's gone through TimeLock. Morgan, I think it can be reversed! Finally. I needed to use some of the old equipment from Genescence, including the original capsules, to test it out. And it seems to be possible, at least in theory. I think I can give you your twenty years back!"

"And I would have been happy with a Cuisinart!"

I laugh at my own dumb joke and give Louis a huge hug. Needless to say, I've prayed for this moment ever since Louis first said it might one day be possible, but nothing could have prepared me for the tsunami of relief and joy I'm feeling right now. Young again . . . a dream come true. And not just for me, but for my beloved friend too.

But something's wrong. Louis is no longer smiling, and in fact, his expression has turned downright grim.

"What's the matter?" I ask tremulously.

"Well, I don't have to tell you that every milk carton at the CIA, Pentagon, and Interpol has Carter Prescott's picture on it. And that he almost certainly has the kalopheen compound from Japan with him."

I nod my head and fear he's about to say exactly what he in fact now says.

"I can't move forward without it."

"There must be more in the world. Where does it come from anyway?"

The jubilation I felt less than a minute ago fades with Louis's response. Turns out kalopheen—which in combination with several other compounds and gamma ray variants stimulates an immediate cellular reaction in humans—can only be found naturally in a remote mountain range in Taliban-controlled Afghanistan. God knows how much Department of Defense funding Prescott siphoned off to broker that particular deal, but there's obviously no way we're packing our bags for Club Kabul anytime soon.

"A little bit goes a long way," Louis says. "That's how Loder was able to keep expanding the TimeLock program. But the original supply ran out long ago, and Prescott no doubt has what's left. Other than what's in the mountains of Afghanistan, at least."

"Okay," I say, trying to reason my way through this formidable setback. "We know President Ayres is desperately trying to track Prescott down but so far, no luck. So let's think—where would he have gone?"

Louis ponders this for a moment, then replies, "Well, he may be persona non grata in America since Myra Winters's ouster, but he's probably still got red, white, and blue blood coursing through his veins. So maybe he's trying to sell his scheme to one of our allies, like England, France, or Germany."

"Maybe," I say. "But my gut says he's gone completely rogue. He knows no rational leader is going to go along with his lunacy, so what if he instead tries to find the highest bidder? Meaning China, North Korea, Iran, or Russia."

"You may be right, but either way, we're out of luck."

Louis's head droops down as low as mine as we realize our hopes of regaining our lost years have likely vanished right along with Carter Prescott forever.

Returning inside the condo, we fill Janine in on our conversation (Kiyoko and Yoshi have known about the possible reversal of the TimeLock process for a while) and she of course shares our boundless frustration in being so close and yet so far from bringing Louis's breakthrough to fruition.

After considering our limited options, we can't help but come to the conclusion that we really don't have any options at all. Prescott could be anywhere in the world at this point, and I'm pretty sure kalopheen isn't one of the suggested gifts on our wedding registry.

Still, I've waited all this time to hear Louis say what he's just said, and he's waited even longer for this possibility, so we're not about to give up now. Because if there's one ironic realization I've come to since I was prematurely aged two years ago, it's that staying hopeful never gets old.

CHAPTER NINETEEN

Although we know Janine and Kiyoko share our desire to track Prescott down, Louis and I have decided to come up with at least a somewhat feasible course of action before bringing up to the topic again to them.

As I sit at a coffee shop corner booth talking conspiratorially with Louis the next morning, I can't help but smile. To everyone else here, we must look like an ordinary father and son possibly discussing the old man's imminent retirement or planning my mom's surprise sixty-fifth birthday party.

It's a given nobody in a million years would guess that the "senior citizen" across from me was in reality born only a few years before I was and that we both played a pivotal role in showing President Myra Winters the door at the White House.

"Okay, let's go through it again," I say. "First, who would want what Prescott has to offer—a weaponized version of TimeLock?"

We look at each other and nod knowingly. Dumb question. At least half the countries in the world would clamor for such an unfair advantage. North Korea, Russia, Iran, China, and Syria come to mind, but virtually any nation with military ambitions and questionable ethics could qualify.

As for the next question—who could afford whatever exorbitant fee Prescott is charging for his services and resources?—the answer leads us to the same players.

And then comes the final question—what would another country need to get Prescott's insane program up to speed?

A lab like the one at Genescence or Hakone, for sure. Easy enough.

A healthy supply of kalopheen; Prescott made off with plenty.

A cold storage facility for the compound, which, as we painfully discovered firsthand back in Hakone, must be kept in a below-freezing environment. No problem.

Extensive security. An absolute certainty—especially since a handful of us, including two amateurs in myself and Yoshi—were able to shut down Prescott's operation in Japan in a matter of hours.

"There's something else they'll need," Louis ventures. "Guinea pigs."

"You're right," I say. "I hadn't thought about it. If they want to fast-track this thing, they'll need test subjects. Lot of them."

"Which makes me think they might take a cue from Loder and use . . ."

"Prisoners."

"Exactly."

"Unfortunately," I add, "that doesn't narrow our list down. Russia, North Korea, China—any of them would round up hundreds of unwitting prisoners for genetic research without thinking twice."

"Which puts us right back at square one. Let's face it, Morgan, there are dozens of highly trained agents around the world unable to find Prescott so far. I'd say the odds of the two of us cracking the case this morning over coffee and muffins are somewhere south of impossible."

"Then maybe we should order something else," I say with a weak smile, trying desperately to bolster our sagging spirits. But then an obvious thought crosses my mind and I add: "We're forgetting the most important resource they'd need to get their program off the ground—you!"

"I don't know about that," Louis says with typical modesty.

"Think about it. Grabbing you, holding Kiyoko—Prescott only went to such extremes because he knew he'd be looking at another five years or more of research without you leading the way."

"Maybe . . ."

"Not maybe. Definitely. Which begs the question—if you were Prescott and needed to quickly replace the esteemed Doctor Lionel Garvey, who would you bring in as back-up pitcher?"

"Well, Emory Layton for starters. But if you're talking somebody on our list of suspect nations, I'd have to say Sergei Baranov, Russia's top cellular geneticist."

Now Louis's eyes open wide with excitement. "Of course! Nobody showed greater interest in TimeLock than Baranov. He and his team must have tried at least a dozen times to steal our research and create a TimeLock program of their own."

Much as I want to share Louis's excitement, the harsh reality is that we're still essentially nowhere. Discovering Russia is Prescott's likely new client isn't much of a revelation and doesn't begin to tell us where in that vast 6.6-million-square-mile country—far and away the largest on the planet—he may be hiding.

CHAPTER TWENTY

Soon after our clandestine coffee shop meeting, Louis and I are filling Janine, Kiyoko, and Yoshi in about our discussion and the possible Sergei Baranov connection. Unfortunately, none of us sees a path forward, especially after Janine calls a CIA buddy and learns that Baranov has been recovering from a knee operation at his Moscow home for weeks, and therefore doesn't appear to be our man after all.

A sense of resignation blankets the room, and I start to pace and mumble. I know it's strange and annoying, but the combo has served me well since childhood, so I continue the ritual. Though I don't look directly at her, I can tell Janine is watching me intently—the only question being whether she's reacting with bemusement at my "charmingly quirky ways" or with amazement that she's promised to say "I do" to this certifiable nut case.

I'll never know because that's when it hits me. "I've got it!" I shout.

The others look on as I sit down and take a deep breath before saying, "We can't find him, but he can find us."

"What are you talking about?" Janine asks.

"Prescott. Let's assume finding him in Russia—or wherever he went—isn't happening. Meaning we can spend years trying to track him down, or we can bring him right to us."

"No way, Morgan," says an anguished Kiyoko. "You're not using Louis as bait. We can't go through that again."

"Not Louis. Me."

"I don't understand," Yoshi chimes in. "Why would Prescott come after you?"

"Because we'll convince him I'd be a valuable commodity. I'm among only a handful of people who went through TimeLock and survived. It worked on me. No side effects. No rapid aging. He studies me, he could jumpstart his program and possibly avoid having another TimeLock debacle on his hands."

"Forget it, Morgan," Janine says forcefully as the others nod in agreement.

"It would be suicide," Louis adds.

"Not necessarily. First, we have Louis send Emory Layton a quote, unquote 'confidential email' all about me. How he's here for my wedding and how happy he is to see I was one of the few who didn't succumb to TimeLock. How I've volunteered to be a test subject for Louis's future genetics studies. How he wished he had someone like me to fast-track his progress during the initial TimeLock trials."

"And how do you know Prescott would see an email like that?" Yoshi asks.

I turn to Louis. "You've always suspected there might be industrial spies monitoring your work. Probably Doctor Layton's, too, since you're both involved in similar research, right?"

Louis nods and I continue: "If these spies are working for Prescott, this would be sure to get their attention and definitely be something they'd want to share with their boss. And if nobody picks up on it, I'll work the deep web and get the word out another way."

"Then we just sit idly by while you're whisked off to God knows where?" asks Kiyoko.

"That's the whole point," I respond. "Not just God, all of you too."

I look over to Janine, knowing this is her area of expertise.

"He means he could have a microchip tracker implanted so we could have eyes on him every step of the way." She shakes her head; her mind is made up. "No way, Morgan! I'm not going to become a widow before I'm even a bride. . . . You know what I mean."

"Morgan, it's all very clever and brave of you," Louis says, "but putting aside the question of your personal safety, Prescott would never go for it in a million years. You're forgetting—he knows you were part of the team that shut down his whole Japanese program and he probably knows how you two deep-faked his beloved Myra Winters out of office. He'd smell a set-up from ten thousand miles away. And emails from me would be red flags for the same reason."

And with that, my head droops. He's right, of course. Janine moves toward me and gives me a comforting hug.

"My hero," she says.

I smile weakly, then stand up and start pacing anew.

"Oh, no," says Yoshi with a smile. "He's doing it again."

But this time my pacing is short-lived. I sit down and gather my thoughts.

"Okay, wrong person, but right idea. I agree with Louis—it can't be me. But what if there was someone else who came through TimeLock unharmed? Older, but unharmed."

"I thought they all died or were murdered," says Janine.

I take out my phone and Google for a minute. Nobody says a word—no doubt afraid to interrupt the crazy man who's seemingly getting loopier by the minute.

"He's alive!"

"Who's alive?" asks Kiyoko.

"Kyle Bannon."

I look around to a sea of blank faces.

"My cellmate at Loomis. Ex-Navy SEAL. He was convicted for a hit-and-run and got fifteen years through TimeLock. But he said he didn't do it."

"Don't they all?" asks Janine.

"Maybe, but sometimes they really didn't do it. *I* didn't."

"Okay," continues Janine, "even if this guy got a raw deal like you did, where do we go with it?"

"When you were temporarily ousted from the FBI, it crushed every fiber of your being. It wasn't a job for you, it was a calling. Working at the agency wasn't just a matter of pride or patriotism, it was at the core of your entire existence."

Janine swallows, temporarily speechless. Finally, this: "Beautifully said, Morgan, and I get it—you're assuming this guy Bannon felt the same way."

"Let's say he really was innocent," I respond. "He goes from a highly trained, proud Navy SEAL to a disgraced convict who's suddenly a middle-aged civilian with no past and very little future."

"So, what are you suggesting, Morgan?" asks Louis before answering his own question. "We find him, see if he wants to be our bait to lure Prescott out of hiding in exchange for . . . what exactly?"

"A full pardon to start."

"Forget it," Janine quickly jumps in. "If he's guilty, his career with the military is over."

"How's this?" I posit. "At the very least, we invite him to take a dip in our little fountain of youth. We give him his fifteen years back. In the meantime, maybe the FBI can look into his case. If it turns out he was wrongly convicted, his record is expunged, his rank is reinstated, and his life is back on track."

There's a long pause as everyone thinks it over. All eyes instinctively turn to Janine, the only law-enforcement pro in the room and the only one here who can ultimately give this longshot Hail Mary plan a thumbs-up or down. Given the risk involved—using a civilian volunteer as prey, possibly launching a raid on a foreign country, going way beyond the purview of the FBI and possibly even the CIA—I'm betting Janine will be forced to put the kibosh on the whole idea. But I quickly realize I've underestimated how willing the "new" Janine is to not always go by the book or even toss it out the window entirely if the cause is worthy enough.

"Here's what we do," she says at last. "Morgan, you and I talk to your guy. If he agrees, I'll launch an investigation into his case with some pals at the Pentagon. We tease out Bannon and see if Prescott bites. Not with emails from Louis—he's right about that raising red flags. But emails from Doctor Layton to someone we'll invent. If Prescott does bite, we track him to wherever they take Bannon, then we organize a rescue team to go in, get him out, bring Prescott and his program down in flames, and bring you boys back the vat of kerosene you need."

Louis and I break into big smiles.

"Kalopheen," we both say in tandem.

"Whatever."

CHAPTER TWENTY-ONE

When I was young—which, despite all appearances to the contrary, wasn't all that long ago—I prided myself on being essentially without prejudice. And up to a point, that was true. I never judged anyone based on their race, gender, cultural background, or sexual orientation.

Or so I thought.

Because one thing I've learned thanks to the new-found "maturity" TimeLock forced upon me is how quick to judgment I actually used to be. That's why I couldn't see past Janine's steely professionalism when I first met her (though, in my defense, she was hauling my ass off to prison at the time), it's why I only saw Louis as a charming but slightly doddering senior citizen when I first met him, and it's why I only saw Kyle Bannon as a brutish central casting redneck when I first met *him*.

Turns out I was wrong on all three counts. And right now, it's Lieutenant Commander Kyle Bannon's turn to show me the error of my ways. Because the imposingly tall, ridiculously fit thirty-year-old "brute" I considered little more than a terrifying walking statue back at Loomis turns out to be a bright, sensitive, and compassionate man who—thanks to the joys of TimeLock—is now pushing fifty, working a dead-end job, and missing his estranged wife and three-year-old daughter every single minute of the day.

Janine and I contacted Bannon a couple of days ago after tracking him down to a run-down section of Philadelphia where he lives in a small apartment and works the night shift at a local gas station mini-mart.

With nothing else going on in his sad, directionless life, Bannon was more than happy to hear from his old roomie and completely receptive to meeting with Janine and me when we mentioned presenting him with what could be a game-changing offer.

Sitting in his drab apartment on this rainy Thursday afternoon, Bannon's eyes open wide with excitement when we fill him in on the plan to lure Prescott out of the shadows. In fact, he's downright giddy—and understandably so. If the mission succeeds, he hopefully gets his fifteen years back, and if, on top of that, the FBI finds exculpatory evidence regarding Bannon's hit and run (he's claimed from the beginning that he was nowhere near the accident site that night), he might just get his record cleared and even be reinstated by the Navy.

"And you want to know what would be the best part?" a smiling Bannon asks.

"Reuniting with your wife and child?" I venture.

"Of course—but I plan on doing that no matter what. No, the best part would be helping bring down that traitorous piece of crap Carter Prescott. Sign me up."

We arrange for Bannon to have a tracker implanted a short time later. The bait is about to be set. The question now is whether Prescott will swim anywhere near it.

CHAPTER TWENTY-TWO

A half dozen seemingly innocuous email exchanges over the next five days between Dr. Emory Layton and the just-invented "noted American geneticist" Dr. Warren Oliver has finally paid off. Deliberately low-key so as to avoid raising any suspicion, the emails mainly focus on Dr. Layton's good fortune in tracking down one Kyle Bannon in Philadelphia and identifying him as one of the very few to have been successfully processed through TimeLock.

Lines like "he'll be an invaluable asset in helping us fully understand the effect of genetic acceleration on the human body" obviously got the attention of Prescott—or at least his team of industrial spies. Because a very brave

Kyle Bannon was in fact grabbed early this morning when a couple of goons showed up as he was about to head home from work.

Naturally, we're all concerned for Bannon's safety, but if anyone is equipped to handle such an ordeal, it's him.

As we wait to get news of his final destination, I finish up for the day in my home office and prepare to head off to join Janine at Louis's hotel. Which, incidentally, is now heavily guarded to prevent another Hakone-like kidnapping from happening again (similar security is in place for Emory Layton, just in case). Almost out the door, I receive a call from Janine, who, in an uncharacteristically worried voice, says, "Stay where you are, Morgan. I'll send a car for you."

"Why? My car's in the garage."

"No! I should have thought of this sooner, but you're much too vulnerable. A perfect target like Kyle. Just wait there."

"I'll be fine. I'll see you in a few."

I hang up and smile—Janine is acting more like a wife than an agent and I love her all the more for it.

Right before getting in my car in our condo's garage, Janine rings me again, but before I can answer a van suddenly screeches to a stop behind me. Three men rush out, grab me, and shove me in the rear cargo area. Within seconds, I'm bound, gagged, and blindfolded, and I realize how we all should have seen this coming. Well, Janine obviously did, but stupid, stubborn, I-know-better-than-a-highly-trained-FBI-agent Morgan obviously didn't. Not only am I another ideal test subject for Prescott, but he can get even with me for helping bring down Sloane Whalen, Myra Winters, and Hakone at the same time.

The van screeches off and I bounce around like the loose cargo I am. Fortunately, though, because my capture went down so quickly, my hosts didn't do a very good job tying me up, so in fairly short order I'm actually able to free my hands. I take off the gag and blindfold and allow myself a brief prideful smile over my Houdini-like escape. Then reality hits and I realize the vehicle is moving far too quickly for me to jump out safely—meaning the only place I can "escape" to is the other side of the van.

Then a longshot gambit occurs to me—a downsized variation of our "car over the mountainside" stunt back in Japan. I move toward a couple of tall boxes in a corner of the back of the van and push one of them toward the rear door. I then open the door, let out a scream, and push the heavy box out onto the dark, vacant road.

As I hoped, my captors have heard the scream and the sound of something—or someone—hitting the pavement, so they bring the van to a shrieking stop. With that, I squeeze myself out of sight behind the other box, praying my literal road show performance will convince my captors that I jumped out the back myself.

All three goons rush to the back of the van, peer in, and then head off down the road. It worked! They'll see the box any second, of course, so I have to get out of here right now. I race out the back and hurry off in the opposite direction of the three men. Running at full speed, I reach for my cell phone only to realize it must have fallen out when they tossed me in the van. Damn. But at least I'm free.

Or am I? Moe, Larry, and Curly apparently just caught on to my ruse and have split up to find me. Though two of the men are headed off in the wrong direction, the remaining one, a tall man with a ridiculously long gait, is closing in on me fast as I run into a wooded area alongside the poorly lit, traffic-less road. I don't think he can see me, but it's likely he's heard me running, so given the disparity in our ages and athletic prowess, it's only a matter of moments before he catches up with me.

Edging ever closer, the man shouts, "I know you're there, Morgan," in an oddly menacing, slasher-movie-worthy, sing-songy voice that rattles me to the core.

I weigh my options and promptly realize I don't have any. The reality is obvious: post-TimeLock, I'm simply in no condition to keep running from my much younger and fitter pursuer, so I come to a stop and ponder my next move. Strange how the mind works, but for a split second, my thoughts hark back to another time I was on the run and ultimately cornered—the morning after Janine and I spent the night together at the River Inn and I was chased and arrested by the cops. Back then, though, I had Janine on hand to rescue me. This time, I'm truly on my own.

With no other recourse, I pick up a heavy chunk of wood, my only chance of knocking this guy down and getting the hell away from here. He's almost here, so I bring my makeshift weapon back like a batter whose only hope of winning the game is to hit a bottom-of-the-ninth grand slam. The man slows down as he nears me, and I can only hope the darkness is preventing him from seeing what I'm about to do. I swing the chunk of wood around toward him with every fiber of strength I have in me, but much to my shock, he casually swirls away in time as if he knew exactly what I was planning. And then I realize that's exactly what happened—he's wearing night vision goggles and has been watching my pathetic little maneuvers every step of the way.

He smiles, points his gun at me, and leads me back to the van like a runaway dog that's about to be sent back to the pound.

I'm shoved into the rear of the van again, but instead of being bound, blindfolded, and gagged this time, one of the henchmen sticks a syringe in my arm, and I can feel myself fading fast. In my few remaining moments of cogent thought, though, I take solace in one comforting fact: Janine and company will soon know where Bannon has been taken and will almost certainly realize I've been invited to join him. At which point a rescue operation will be mounted and my nightmarish association with TimeLock will truly be over forever.

CHAPTER
TWENTY-THREE

The first sensation I feel is cold. Bitter, bracing cold. I open my eyes and see the reason why—just outside of the small room I'm in is a seemingly endless vista of snow. Snow on the ground, snow on the mountains beyond, snow falling from the sky, and snow landing atop what seems to be—or are the drugs they pumped into me messing with my mind?—a rocket launcher.

I tentatively rise, my thoughts muddled and my movements hesitant. To my horror, a sense of déjà vu creeps over me as I realize this is exactly how I felt stepping out of the TimeLock capsule two years ago. Not surprisingly, the door to my room—cell, more accurately—is locked, and for a moment it feels like I'm back at Loomis. Jesus—Loomis! Is Kyle Bannon holed up in the next cell, and where in God's name are we, anyway?

I don't have to wait long for an answer as moments later two very large and decidedly humorless gentlemen remove me from my cell, push me out a side door, and seat me in the sidecar of a motorcycle. As we ride off, I look back toward the gray, run-down building where I had been held and spot an outdoor area populated by what looks like prisoners surrounded by a dozen or so armed guards.

We pass several abandoned rocket launchers as well as other vestiges of what was clearly some sort of space research facility. Only this one definitely wasn't run by NASA. In fact, I recognize the writing on the equipment as Russian.

Last thing I remember, I was a middle-aged American cybersecurity consultant; now all of a sudden, I'm Dr. Zhivago.

I'm taken into a recently (and hastily) constructed building and shoved into a large office. My two "hosts" leave, and a moment later, I'm greeted by a formidable man of about fifty-five with the requisite chiseled features and imposing height of a seasoned military leader. I recognize him instantly as Brigadier General Carter Prescott.

"Hello, Morgan. Welcome." Prescott says in a counter-intuitively polite tone that reminds me of Patrick Loder.

"Welcome to where?"

"I doubt you've heard of it, but we're in the province of Magadan in northeastern Siberia near the Sea of Okhotsk."

"Terrific," I say. "I've always wanted to visit here. Any restaurant suggestions?"

Prescott ignores my juvenile gallows humor and says, "I trust you had a good flight."

"The best kind. I slept through the whole thing."

"Drink?"

Prescott pours a couple of brandies. I take a sip and force myself to keep this conversation as calm and pseudo-friendly as possible, especially since I know things will get ugly for me as soon as the pleasantries are done. I desperately want to ask him about Bannon, but can't let on that I've been in touch with him since Loomis.

"Let me answer your questions, Morgan. First, what is this place? Well, as you've seen, it used to be a space research facility run by an agency called Roscosmos, Russia's equivalent of NASA. The temperature and remote location proved unsuitable for the agency's needs, but ideal for mine, so I set up shop here a few weeks ago."

"Hakone redux, I take it?"

"Yes, well, you and your friends did manage to throw a monkey wrench into that one, didn't you?" he says, again with an oddly calm voice that somehow frightens me more than the expected screaming and fist-banging.

"And I was brought here why?" I ask, though I already know the answer.

"You slowed down my plans in Japan, but I think you might just be able to speed them up here."

"I got a C in science, General. Not sure what help I can be."

"It's not your mind that interests me, Morgan."

"That's what she said."

"It's your DNA. You and only a handful of inmates managed to avoid the TimeLock curse. Something in your immune system enabled the process to work as planned. In fact, your former cellmate was one of the other lucky ones, so he's joined us here as well."

Thank God—Bannon is alive, which also means a rescue team should be on their way right now.

"So you're going to poke and prod us until you've learned all you can and then we disappear into some Siberian snowbank forever, right?"

Prescott doesn't answer because the answer is obvious. He pours us another drink.

"You're really a sick fuck, Prescott. A traitor and a murderer. It's all about power for you, isn't it? Even if you have to sell out your own country to get it."

Smart move, Morgan! Real bright. Just when we were getting along so well. I brace myself for Prescott's inevitable fury, but instead of being angry, he produces a strange smile.

"You've seen too many spy movies, Morgan. You think you have it all figured out, right? Because in the movies, this is where the villain would throw this glass against the wall and start screaming how he didn't betray America—America betrayed him! And now they'll all pay for what they did to me. Sound about right?"

Sounds exactly right, in fact. Okay, I'm not sure where he's going with this, but it's definitely not where I expected.

"I get it. You think I'm some crazed warmonger who would do anything to destroy the enemy. That was Myra. That was Sloane. Their intentions were noble, but their thinking was one-dimensional. All they wanted was victory over an opponent. What I want is victory over war itself."

"What are you talking about?"

"Let me tell you a little about myself," Prescott says.

If telling me his life story will delay whatever nightmares he has in store for all of us, then I hope he signs on to Ancestry.com and traces his entire family history for me.

"It's 2012 and I'm in Afghanistan," Prescott begins. "My second tour of duty and I was already a Command Sergeant. Operation Enduring Freedom was in its eleventh year and I would continue to serve for as long as they needed me there. And not to be too immodest, but I was a walking recruitment poster for military service—the son of a general and the latest in a long line of high-ranking Army heroes. Like them, I aspired to be both commanding and fearless—an inspiring leader among those who ranked below me and a rising star among those who ranked above me."

I'd hate to hear how he describes himself when he's *not* worried about being immodest.

"It was a brutally hot day in Paktia. What else, right? *Every* day was a brutally hot day in Paktia."

I nod in agreement as if I'm recalling my own brutally hot days in Paktia, a place I never heard of until five seconds ago.

"My team had been engaged in on-and-off skirmishes with the Taliban all day," Prescott continues. "But calm had finally settled over our unit, that unnerving yet scintillating wartime quiet that we all knew could either be welcome relief after a brutal day of fighting or the proverbial calm before the storm in advance of an all-out enemy assault. Well, as it happened, the calm didn't last long. At exactly nine, the sound of machine guns and rockets shattered the tenuous silence and all hell broke loose.

"Five members of my squad were killed instantly and we promptly eliminated at least a dozen enemy soldiers seconds later. The back-and-forth seemed to last forever, but by nine thirty, the fight had come down to five survivors from each side facing off on a hillside. If it wasn't for the advanced weaponry we were all pointing at each other, the scene might have been from a Civil War musket stand-off or even a sword fight between the Romans and the Celts in the late fourth century."

Prescott smiles knowingly and I try to do the same—two friends reminiscing about their war years. But then his smile gives way to a thoughtful seriousness and I immediately follow suit.

"For a brief moment—a moment I'll never forget—ten young men, who in peacetime might have been on the way to dinner or a concert, stood staring at each other with hate and fear. A hate forged by political leaders who quite likely would never themselves step foot on a battlefield in their lives, and a fear borne of the certainty that these might well be their last moments on Earth. And for eight of them, they were. Guns were fired and men dropped to the barren, dusty ground. Only one of my men and I survived, but there was another casualty that fateful night, Morgan. My once-unflappable support of war.

"Until that night and until that moment, I had of course seen too much death and destruction not to consider war a tragic abomination. But I simply couldn't deny one harsh reality: there was a part of me that saw combat not only as honorable, but, God forgive me, exhilarating. The excitement, the patriotism, the loyalty, the camaraderie, the nobility of vanquishing an enemy—all of these sensibilities were so wired into my DNA that I ironically felt more alive in the shadow of death and destruction than at any other time in my life."

Prescott pours us another drink, then goes on: "After that night in Paktia, though, I became obsessed with the idea of preventing war rather than engaging in it. Hadn't the United States and Russia, for example, somehow managed to avoid serious confrontations for decades thanks to the concept of mutual assured destruction? Why, then, couldn't the same concept work when it came to non-nuclear warfare? And then, once I returned to the States, I found two kindred spirits—Sloane Whalen and Myra Winters. And here we are."

I pause for a second, trying to be as careful with my words as possible, lest I say the wrong thing and hasten my own inevitable demise.

"To be honest, I'm not sure I follow."

"Sure you do, Morgan. Think about it. The program we started in Japan has always been about finding a way to diminish an enemy combatant's speed, stamina, strength, and mental clarity on the battlefield, right? All through instantaneous cellular degradation. TimeLock 2.0, you might say. I get it; to you, it's complete madness. But that's the whole point of it. Don't you see, Morgan? I never wanted this program just for America or just for Russia. I want *everyone* to have it one day, because when they do, *nobody* will have an advantage and maybe they won't start the fucking war in the first place."

"Conventional warfare's answer to mutual assured destruction."

"Yes! Yes! I knew you'd understand. Can't you see, Morgan—you're not James Bond, I'm not Blofeld, and this place isn't my secret lair. Sure, it can get messy and it can get bloody, but I'm actually trying to do the right thing here."

I'll admit it—I'm surprised. Much like I was when Kyle Bannon turned out to be far more complicated than he seemed at first glance. Nevertheless, however unexpected Prescott's motivations may be, he's still quite mad. Where he believes that a weaponized TimeLock will bring ground combat to an end, I believe it will only open the floodgates for deadlier biological, or even nuclear, warfare. Where he believes sharing his findings with the world will create an even playing field, I believe it will prompt countries like North Korea and Russia to try to crush enemy nations before they know what hit them.

Knowing I'll never change his mind, though, I decide not to press any of these points. Most of all, I need to stay on his good side—relatively speaking—until the rescue team arrives.

But there's one issue I can't ignore.

"The building you're keeping me in. When your men were bringing me here, I noticed it had a yard crowded with prisoners. I take it these are the other guinea pigs for your research?"

"Before you waste your pity on them, keep in mind they were prisoners before being transferred here. Whatever happens to them is well deserved."

"Living in squalor? Freezing to death? Being experimented on? Are you trying to bring the gulags back, General?"

"There is no progress without sacrifice, Morgan. And if your pal Garvey had cooperated, we may not have needed these so-called guinea pigs in the first place."

Which gives me an opening I quickly take. "Correct me if I'm wrong, General Prescott, but unless you went through ten years of medical school in the last year, you're not conducting these experiments yourself."

Prescott hesitates for a moment.

"Come on, General. You can tell me. Remember, this is the part where you spill all the details of your evil plan because I'll be dead soon anyway."

Prescott smiles. "Not that the name would mean anything to you, but a certain Doctor Sergei Baranov—Russia's leading genetics expert—has joined the team. All very hush-hush, of course. In fact, we have a decoy at his home near Moscow pretending to be him recovering from a knee operation."

So we were right about Baranov after all. Which means Special Forces will be able to take down not only Carter Prescott, but perhaps the one man who could bring this project to fruition other than the esteemed Dr. Lionel Garvey. Which of course begs the question that's been swirling in my mind since Prescott confirmed that Kyle Bannon was here as well: How long will it be until our rescuers arrive?

The answer for that will have to wait, of course, so I again decide my best course of action is to keep Prescott talking as long as possible. In fact, I'm about to ask him to tell me some of his other wartime adventures when he suddenly stands up and gestures for me to do the same. Our civil conversation is apparently over, and, much as I hate to show any weakness to this professional predator, I can't help but start shaking, not only from the frigid weather but from the escalating terror.

"Well, thanks for the drinks and the chat," I manage to say. "Maybe we can catch a movie next time."

Prescott produces a small smile at my second dumb attempt at humor and says, "You go get a good night's sleep, Morgan. You've got a busy day tomorrow."

Watching the Special Forces team drop your sorry ass into the Sea of Okhotsk, I hope.

CHAPTER
TWENTY-FOUR

After my little tête-à-tête with Prescott, I'm returned to the prison facility. Apparently, my first-class privileges have been revoked, because I'm no longer placed in a private cell but instead shown to a bunk in a large grim room where at least fifty other prisoners are crowded together. Because I missed the "dinner hour" during my time with Prescott, I'm given a stale sandwich, which I pray doesn't start moving. I gobble it down in a matter of seconds.

I look around the room in despair. I'm used to being around prisoners, thanks to my staycation at Loomis, but this feels entirely different. There's no pretense toward civilization here because there's no pretense that these men will ever be released. And while I'm sure some of them more than deserve incarceration, what they're being subjected to here is closer to barbarism. And then there's the very real possibility that many of these men aren't here because they committed some heinous crime; they're here because they dared to speak up against their oppressive government.

There's something else I can't help but notice. At Loomis, most of the men at least feigned an air of resolve, a conviction, if you'll forgive the pun, that one day they'd be free again. Here, though, it's impossible to see anything but defeatism—the absolute certainty that their fates are sealed and their lives are over.

Heartbreaking though it is to take in this bastion of hopelessness, nothing rattles me more than spotting the young man I see curled up in a cot a few yards from me. Because he's not even a young man, he's a boy. Probably in his mid-teens at most, he reminds me of myself when I was that age. Which, I keep reminding myself, wasn't all that long ago.

Something about this unfortunate boy prompts me to risk the wrath of the guards by sneaking toward his cot and offering him the bag of chips they also left for me. He looks at me in both fear and curiosity—what does this strange middle-aged man want with me?

"I'm not hungry," I lie. "Please take it."

"I can't pay," he says in halting but decent English. "No money, no cigarettes."

"No problem," I say. "Your English is good."

"Studied in school."

"My name is Morgan Eberly."

"Mikhail Evanoff."

"Hey, we have the same initials," I say with a smile, but he doesn't seem to understand. We shake hands and then he opens the bag of chips and wolfs them down.

"Why are you here, Mikhail?"

"Taken with my father. He stole some food and they arrested both of us."

"Is he here?"

"He was."

"He's dead?"

"Bad reaction to medicine," he says, his voice cracking with emotion. "I was with him. The room wasn't cold but suddenly he turned blue like he was freezing. A minute later he was gone."

157

Mikhail is clearly doing everything he can to hold back his tears and for his sake, I'm desperately trying to hold back my own.

"What do they want from us?" he asks.

"I don't know." Another lie, but I see no point in making him more terrified than he already is. "But I might be able to get you out of here soon." The second I say this, I regret it. I have no idea if I can trust this kid, and, if I can, I have no right building up his hopes for an escape that may never happen.

"How?" he asks.

No turning back now. "Because my friends in America know we're here and are coming to rescue us."

"Why you want help me?"

"Let's just say I was also sent to prison for something I didn't do when I was a young man. How old are you anyway?"

"Thirteen." He's even younger than I thought.

"I was twenty-three. Seems like yesterday. Do you have any other family?"

"My mother died a long time ago. I have cousin in Poland but he was adopted by a family after his parents were killed by a rival gang."

158

Good God. What this poor kid has been through makes my ordeal seem tame by comparison. "Well, I'll do everything I can to get you out."

"I miss my father."

"I lost mine when I was in my teens too, so we have a lot in common, don't we?"

He nods uncertainly, still no doubt wondering if there are insidious ulterior motives for all the attention I'm paying him.

It's time for me to leave. "Nice to meet you, Mikhail. Don't tell anyone what I told you about the Americans coming, okay?"

"Of course. Good night, Morgan."

"Good night."

I climb back in what could laughingly be called my bed and start to doze off when I hear my name again: "Morgan!"

I look up and am elated to see Kyle Bannon crouched down (not easy when you're six-foot-five) and heading my way. I get up and we give each other a bear hug— strangers in a strange land who've suddenly become brothers in arms.

"What the hell are you doing here?" Kyle asks.

"Same as you. Why settle for one TimeLock graduate when you can have two? I should have seen it coming."

"I assume Agent Price knows you're here?"

"Well, I wasn't with her when they took me, but I'm sure she figured it out. In fact, she tried to warn me but I didn't listen. So, when do you think they'll get here?"

"Assuming they've been tracking me this whole time, it won't be tonight," Kyle says. "Too soon and it's not like they can just do a fly-over without being spotted. Lucky for us, we're near the water, so I'm guessing they'll launch a chopper assault from sea."

"Which they'd never do during the day, so we're looking at tomorrow night at the earliest, right?"

"Looks that way," Kyle responds.

"So all we have to do is survive tomorrow."

"You got it." He pauses a second, then adds: "Hey, Morgan?"

"Yeah."

"I want to thank you."

"Very funny."

"No, I'm serious. We're deep in the shits right now, but I'm betting we get out of this. And when we do, I might actually have a life to go back to because of you guys. So, like I said, thank you, man."

"You're welcome, but I think you got it wrong. We should be thanking *you*. After all, I was a careless and unwilling participant, but you actually volunteered for this crazy mission. You know what that makes you, right?"

"One dumb fuck?"

"I was going to say brave, but one dumb fuck works too."

We exchange smiles, then hear a guard headed our way. Kyle scampers back to his bunk and fifteen minutes later, I'm finally able to block out the incessant snoring of fifty exhausted, undernourished, and terrified men, and drift off to sleep.

CHAPTER
TWENTY-FIVE

After a delightful morning repast of powdered eggs and three-day-old bread, a bunch of us are taken to the medical building and then separated into smaller groups. As we pass through the main hallway, I peak inside some of the rooms to see several men being forced into glass-enclosed chambers and doused with a reddish spray of some kind. Some of the men are screaming, some are pounding on the glass, and all of them are consumed with terror.

The only bright spot of my morning is peering down a hallway to see a room with a prominent hazard symbol depicting a snowflake on the door, then spotting two men wearing what appear to be protective suits designed to ward off the cold. I make a mental note of the exact location since this is almost certainly where the kalopheen is being stored—a cold storage room like the one we hid in back in Hakone.

Now I'm taken to a smaller room with a single bed, lots of medical equipment, and several large-screen monitors. I sit alone for a few minutes until the door opens and a striking looking man walks in. Louis showed me his picture, so I recognize the forty-year-old Sergei Baranov right away. Looking like some Russian matinee idol, Baranov is chiseled, handsome, and supremely confident. I can't stand him already.

"Doctor Mengele, I presume," I say.

When will I learn not to antagonize my captors? Baranov casually walks up to me and promptly punches me in the stomach. I double over in pain and do everything in my power not to give him the satisfaction of seeing me crumple to the floor.

"Never, ever, compare me to that monster again. I thought General Prescott explained to you—our work here is in the name of peace."

"I guess all the screaming fooled me," I manage to say.

"Science is trial and error, Mister Eberly. The temporary discomfort of a few lowlifes is meaningless compared to the global good that might come out of it. But since you're so concerned with the welfare of our other guests here, take solace in the fact that you and your friend Bannon alone might provide all the answers we need."

"Then let's get on with it," I say with all the fake bravado I can muster.

Unlike the other prisoners here, I'm spared the horror of being assaulted by sprays and gases—at least for now. Instead, my day—and I'm assuming Kyle's as well—is spent giving blood, having a fairly routine physical exam, and then being run through several MRI-like devices, all of which bring back the terror I felt climbing into the TimeLock capsule back when all this started.

Five hours later, I'm back in my prison barracks where Kyle and I, with my new young friend Mikhail watching from a few yards away, are all seated on benches in front of long tables and served what I can only assume is, was, or at one time aspired to be some kind of meat. But it isn't just the dinner that's hard to swallow—it's the possibility of having to stay here a single day more.

CHAPTER TWENTY-SIX

Sometime in the middle of the night, I'm awaked by the sound of helicopters and gunfire. Also known as music to my ears—our rescue team is here!

Moments later, a half dozen Special Forces team members burst into our barracks, and while the Russian prisoners understandably retreat from these gun-bearing intruders, Kyle and I make our way toward them. The men seem to recognize us from their planning briefings, but we identify ourselves just in case.

"Second Lieutenant Reilly," says one of the men as he hands Kyle an M4 carbine fitted with laser and night vision sights. He then hands me a Glock 19 and says, "You know how to use this?" and I nod. Well, nod-*ish*, since what little I know comes from Janine's standard issue from the FBI.

"How many of you?" Kyle asks.

"Twenty-three. The others are securing the main housing facility where we assume Prescott is."

"Janine Price. Is she with you?" I ask.

"Right here, soldier boy."

As if she waited to make her big cinematic entrance, Janine, in full fatigues, steps out of the shadows and we run into each other's arms.

"I should have known you'd be leading the operation!" I say with a beaming smile on my face.

"Not leading," says Janine. "Just participating. Not exactly FBI purview. But I suddenly had a craving for Siberian food and thought, what the hell."

As Janine warmly greets and thanks Kyle, I chime in with this to Janine and Lt. Reilly: "There's a cold storage facility in a northwest corridor on the first floor of the medical building. Can I get one of your men to go there with me? Precious cargo we need to keep out of Russian hands."

"We know all about it, Mister Eberly," Reilly responds. Of course they do—she may not formally be running the show, but this is definitely a Janine Price operation.

"What about the prisoners here?" Reilly asks. "We can't hold them."

"Let them escape," I respond. "I'd say they've served their time." I look over to Janine and she nods in agreement.

"Okay, I have a team member who speaks Russian. Sergeant Jackson will deal with them. Let's go."

"Wait, Lieutenant. I need a favor." I spot Mikhail across the room and beckon him toward me. He reluctantly approaches.

"Lieutenant, this is Mikhail. He has vital information about Prescott's other contacts in Russia and I want to take him back to the States with us."

Reilly and Janine look at me skeptically. What "vital information" could this kid possibly have? But Mikhail picks up on my expression and wisely jumps in with this: "I got assignment because I'm seventeen but look like boy. I just want to help U.S. of A."

Reilly is still unsure but doesn't have time to argue the point given the urgency of the mission at hand. "Fine. I'll turn him over to Sergeant Jackson. Go!"

I high-five Mikhail and give a thumbs-up to a thoroughly perplexed Janine.

"I'm going with you," she shouts.

"No, I've got this," I respond. "Just make sure Prescott and Baranov don't get away."

Janine nods and runs off as I do the same with Sergeant Fowler, who is assigned to accompany me to the cold storage facility to retrieve the kalopheen. A few minutes later, he and I are pleasantly surprised to discover how easy the medical facility is to penetrate, but our relief is quickly shattered when a hail of bullets crash all around us once we're inside, thanks to two guards working the night shift.

Sergeant Fowler is able to shoot both of them in short order, and I turn to him and say, "Well done, Sergeant. Thank you!" But there's no response. And how can there be? Fowler is on the floor, having been hit upon entry. Fearing the worst, I lean down, put my ear to his chest and am beyond relieved to find he's alive. His eyes open, he points to his shoulder and smiles—he'll be alright. I now hear the sound of footsteps running in a nearby hall and Fowler gestures—go!

Gun drawn, I start running as well—not to catch up with whomever else is in the building, but to make my way to the supply of kalopheen and get the hell out of here. Breathless, I finally enter the cold storage room, which more than lives up to its name and—like its counterpart back in Hakone—is absolutely freezing. There are rows and rows of test tubes filled with liquids of every color under the sun, but fortunately Louis has told me exactly which one to look for. Dark green and marked K27HP.

Except nothing matching that description is anywhere to be found.

Seconds later, I realize why.

"This what you're looking for, Mister Eberly?" says Sergei Baranov as he emerges from a back corner of the room, a gun in one hand, and a large metal case in the other. "Drop your weapon."

"Funny, I was going to ask you to do the same thing."

"I'm afraid you're at a bit of a disadvantage," Baranov responds. "If you fire from that position and hit anything but me, you'll set off a chemical reaction that will kill us both."

He's right. If I miss, I'm almost certain to hit one of the banks of test tubes and gas canisters and that's all she wrote. I lower my weapon and see that Baranov is pointing his. No way I'm getting out of here if I give up now. It's all-or-nothing time, so I suddenly lift the Glock up and shoot out the overhead light fixture.

With the room plunged into darkness, Baranov fires off a couple of shots but misses me. I barrel toward him and push him to the ground, prompting him to drop his gun. Unable to retrieve his weapon, Baranov scrambles to his feet and races off. I forget about killing or capturing him, grab the metal case, and bolt out of the room and then out of the building.

CHAPTER
TWENTY-SEVEN

I'm hurrying toward the housing facility with the case in hand when I spot Mikhail running in another direction. I yell after him but he doesn't hear me. What in the world could he be doing?

Though I shouldn't deviate from the plan—especially for a kid I've known for only two days—I decide to follow him. Partly out of concern, partly out of curiosity, and partly because I see so much of myself in this lost young man coping at the same time with the loss of his father *and* the loss of his freedom.

I'm assuming Mikhail is headed back to the prison barracks for some reason, but then he surprises me by running right past the building. But in pursuit of what? I continue to shout for him to stop but he doesn't hear me or pretends not to. Either way, I'm in no shape to keep up with a thirteen-year-old boy, so it's only a matter of time before I lose him.

But thanks to the lights from the barracks, I now see what I couldn't see before. Mikhail is chasing after none other than Baranov—the man who killed his father. It appears to me that Baranov doesn't even know he's being chased, he's simply trying to get away. I can only pray it stays that way because if Mikhail tries to go one-on-one with the incredibly fit Baranov, he won't last ten seconds.

Just now, I spot a true godsend—one of the complex's numerous motorcycles. My favorite form of transportation! I hot-wire it, stow the case in the rear cargo box, climb aboard, and race toward Mikhail. Well, not race exactly—this thing is so old I'm surprised Fred Flintstone isn't pedaling it—but it's certainty faster than I am, and a few minutes later I catch up to my young friend and we both come to a stop.

"Mikhail, forget about him. We have a strict timetable and need to get out of here."

"You go ahead, Morgan. That bastard killed my father. You have gun?"

I do, but there's no way I'm handing it over to him. But another thought crosses my mind—I have no desire to let Baranov get away either.

"Listen to me, Mikhail. You go back to Sergeant Fowler and Lieutenant Reilly at the main housing building. Tell them I've gone after Baranov and to give me fifteen minutes before they take off. You understand?"

"I go with you."

"No. I can't allow that. I'll take care of Baranov. I promise."

Mikhail thinks it over for a few seconds, then finally nods. He gives me a thumbs-up and runs back toward the housing facility. I rev the engine and ride off in pursuit of Baranov, who's off in the distance running away from the complex and up a hill. Two minutes later, I'm closing in on him. Given that he isn't shooting at me, I assume he's still unarmed, so for the time being I have the advantage. He pauses at the top of the hill as I dismount, gun in hand.

"It's all over, Doctor," I say. "You're coming with me."

"To face a life behind bars in an American penitentiary?"

"At least you'll get a fair trial, which is more than you deserve."

"Your memory appears to be failing you, Mister Eberly. As I recall, you wouldn't have lost decades of your life to TimeLock if *you* had received a fair trial. So perhaps your American justice system isn't quite as just as you'd like to believe."

"TimeLock is dead and so is your program, Baranov. Let's go."

"Thank you for the offer, but I'll have to respectfully decline."

With which Baranov runs over the crest of a hill and into the darkness. I immediately give chase and follow him down the other side of the hill where I hear the sound of water growing louder and louder. This has to end now, so I start shooting, but in the darkness it's almost impossible to get a fix on him. Just then, however, I get lucky—Baranov climbs a short distance to the top of another hill, comes to a stop, and raises his arms in surrender.

I cautiously head toward him with my gun pointed straight at his head. He gives me a smile as if to say, "you got me," and I'm ready to bask in the victory of his capture when he suddenly hurls himself over the edge of the hill. I fire, but it's too late. I run toward the edge and look down on a wide river flowing powerfully toward the sea. I wait for Baranov to come up for air if he's alive, or for his body to float down river if he isn't, but neither happens.

He's gone, and so is my chance of bringing him to justice.

CHAPTER
TWENTY-EIGHT

A few minutes later, I ride the motorcycle up toward the housing facility where I see three moderately wounded Special Forces men being treated by a medic. I'm happy to then see Sergeant Fowler make his way toward them and likewise receive first aid. I ask one of the men where Janine is, and he gestures toward the main building—she's gone after Prescott. I'm about to join her when I spot Mikhail safely hidden behind an old rocket launcher. As I walk toward him, I think it over and make my decision.

"You get Baranov?" Mikhail asks hopefully.

"I caught up with him," I say—technically the truth if not the whole story.

"Good work, Morgan," Mikhail smiles with relief. "Where is he?"

"Gone. In the river," I tell him. "You don't have to worry about him anymore."

"Thank you for me and for my papa," a choked-up Mikhail says.

I hate feeding Mikhail this lie of omission, but I'll always believe I did the right thing—especially since it's entirely possible Baranov did in fact perish in that river. Instead of spending the rest of his days consumed by anger and vengeance, he'll hopefully be able to start a new life comforted by the belief that his father's death has been avenged.

I tell Mikhail to stay put and out of the line of fire, and I find a slightly injured Lieutenant Reilly.

"You alright?" I ask him.

"Nothing serious."

"Kyle with Janine?"

Reilly nods. "Once we have Prescott, we set the charges, and hightail it out of here."

"I have to help."

"There's nothing you can do. Stay here where it's safe."

"That would, of course, be the smart thing to do," I say right before moving toward the housing building. "Unfortunately, Lieutenant, I'm not that bright."

I open the metal case to find about fifty vials all marked K27HP and ask the medic to keep a close eye on the precious cargo. I run inside the building and take in the carnage—Prescott's guards litter the floor. I now hear gunfire from another corner of the building and run toward it. I hurry into an industrial-sized kitchen to find Carter Prescott standing in a corner as Janine and Kyle and five Special Forces operatives—all with guns drawn—close in on him.

Janine glares at me—what am I doing in the line of fire yet again? But Kyle gives me a warm squeeze on the shoulder. As I move forward, Prescott spots me and with a knowing half smile on his face, says to me and Janine: "You two are starting to become a real thorn in my side."

"Maybe you can pull a few strings in DC and get a cell next to Myra Winters," Janine responds.

"There'll be no cell, Agent Price, because there'll be no trial. I've decided to be my own judge, jury, and executioner."

I lurch forward as I realize what Prescott is doing. He's taken out a small capsule from his shirt pocket and swallows it. His eyes open wide, and he collapses to the floor.

Janine crouches down and confirms that Prescott is dead.

"Let's get out of here!" Kyle shouts and we head off, but not before I take one last look back at Prescott. I shake my head in both fury and even a small touch of sadness for such a once-noble life gone so horribly wrong.

We regroup with Reilly and his team. I grab hold of the metal case and beckon Mikhail over as we all rush to the choppers. Janine fills Reilly in on the demise of Prescott and, out of Mikhail's earshot, I tell him I honestly don't know what became of Sergei Baranov. Reilly in turns tells us his men have just finished wiring the place—all excepting the prison barracks. As for the prisoners, some might stay, some might run, but none will be subjected to what Prescott and Baranov have put them through ever again.

Ten minutes later, we're all on board four choppers, and we lift off. As we do, huge explosions go off below us. First, the medical building, then the housing facility, then finally the executive offices.

I look down to see three dozen or so prisoners running off into the distance, and for the first time in days

I feel what they must be feeling—hopeful, relieved, and at long last, free.

CHAPTER
TWENTY-NINE

It's a few days later, and we're back home in America, the ordeal of Magadan, Siberia, officially behind us. On the flight back, I had asked Janine if she thought Russia might retaliate militarily for America's unauthorized Special Forces raid on their sovereign land. Much to my surprise, though, she informed me that the powers that be in the Kremlin had actually clandestinely supported the operation, obviously hoping as much as we did to keep Baranov and Prescott's insane chemical warfare research program buried forever.

How ironic if those two madmen may actually have inadvertently brokered a tenuous détente between our two adversarial nations.

No less surprisingly was this additional unexpected revelation from Janine: Walter Greene, Mr. Conventionality himself, was actually the one who made the decidedly unconventional decision to allow Janine to take part in the raid in Siberia. Could it be that even a man as firmly set in his ways as Walter Greene has actually evolved over the past two years, much as Janine and I have?

What will become of our junior team member Mikhail has yet to be determined, but an idea keeps running through my head. For now, all I know is that this lost yet resourceful boy who's currently in transitional immigration custody has had a profound effect on me. Not simply because we both lost our fathers around the same age or even that we both found ourselves imprisoned for crimes we didn't commit. But because he's tapped into a powerful paternal instinct in me I never knew I had until recently. Before TimeLock, the thought would never have crossed my mind, but now I think about it constantly—I can't wait to be a father. After all, I'm not getting any younger, am I?

It's a few days later and Janine and I are at the GenQuest Bio-Tech processing facility along with Louis, Kiyoko, Yoshi, and Dr. Layton. You guessed it—the moment of truth is finally here, and I'd be lying if I told you I wasn't shaking with both anxiety and anticipation. In a few minutes, I'll be voluntarily reliving the worst moment of my life other than the loss of my dad—climbing into a TimeLock capsule. Louis is no less excited and nervous, as is Dr. Layton.

Insisting that he go first, Louis climbs into one of the capsules, no doubt remembering how horribly wrong it went for him the last time he put himself through. The capsule closes and begins gliding along the tracks. A fine spray of the kalopheen we brought back from Russia begins pumping in, and we watch on the monitor. And then we watch some more.

Nothing. It isn't working!

A minute or so later, Dr. Layton shuts down the process and a grim Louis climbs out. He knows something's wrong but doesn't realize the reversal completely failed until he sees his reflection in the control room glass and sees the familiar vestiges of time on his face and the dejected expressions of bitter disillusionment on ours.

"Damn it!" he shouts. "I don't understand."

We all move toward him, and I put a comforting hand on his shoulder.

"You tried, Louis. I guess it just wasn't meant to be."

"I don't accept that, Morgan. It should have worked."

Louis walks toward the control panel and Dr. Layton joins him. Janine squeezes my arm wordlessly—the appropriate gesture considering there are no words she could possibly summon that would alleviate our crushing disappointment.

Now Louis unwittingly imitates my oft-ridiculed pacing routine by beginning a pacing ritual of his own that would almost be comical if any of us felt even the slightest bit jovial. But no one dares derail his train of thought—even Dr. Layton, the only person here who might be able to offer an educated guess as to what went wrong.

After a few long minutes, Louis opens his eyes wide, struck by some revelation much as I was when I figured out his brilliant Winters/Hakone clues back in Japan.

"Lionel, what it is?" Dr. Layton asks excitedly.

"I didn't allow for a possible modification."

"Of course," Dr. Layton responds as the rest of us look on cluelessly. Then realizing Kiyoko, Yoshi, Janine, and I are completely in the dark, Louis turns to us and says, "I'm such a fool. I should have realized that Baranov would have modified his supply of kalopheen to undertake his experiments."

Off our confused looks, Dr. Layton explains, "What I think Lionel is saying is that in order to develop an easily transmissible variation of the original TimeLock formula, Baranov would need to have altered the molecular structure of the kalopheen in his possession."

"Meaning," Louis chimes in, "we're dealing with a whole new strain that may never serve our purposes."

"Can't you analyze what was brought back from Russia and determine what the modification was?" Janine asks.

"I can try, but there are so many variables it could take weeks or months, and by that time, the kalopheen will have degraded."

Louis turns to me forlornly and says in a sad, soft voice, "We may really be out of luck this time, Morgan. I'm so sorry. If only I had been there with you in Siberia, I might have figured out what Baranov was up to."

Again, Louis begins to pace and I instinctively do the same. We must look to the others like we've just decided to form a TimeLock marching band. We continue our mini-parade for a couple of minutes, but then it's my turn for the proverbial light bulb to go off.

"I just remembered," I say excitedly. "Mikhail was in the lab with Baranov. He told me he was spared because the prisoner who they experimented on before him died. His father."

"I'm not sure how that helps us," Dr. Layton comments.

"I'm not sure how either," I respond. "But does this mean anything to the two of you: he said the room was warm but his father suddenly turned blue and somehow actually froze to death in a matter of seconds."

Louis and Dr. Layton exchange glances and at the same instant, shout, "Cryomolecularization!!"

"Just what I was thinking," I deadpan.

"What is it, Louis?" Janine asks.

"Baranov must have frozen the kalopheen far beyond its normal subzero temperature to enhance its efficacy," Louis says. "That's why it had such an immediate impact on Mikhail's poor father. But, knowing that, I think I know what I need to do to make this work!"

Janine, Kiyoko, and I share big smiles and retreat to the next room while our two Mensa-worthy geneticists do their thing. Two agonizingly tense hours later, a beaming Louis and Dr. Layton walk in and nod in unison—problem solved.

CHAPTER THIRTY

An hour later, we again watch Louis's capsule slowly glide along. This time, however, the transformation begins almost immediately, and over the next few minutes, the elderly Dr. Lionel Garvey morphs before our eyes into the thirty-eight-year-old Louis Garrett, a man Janine and I have only seen in photographs, but whom Kiyoko fell in love with all those years ago.

Three minutes later and it's done. The capsule opens and Dr. Layton, myself, and Yoshi help Louis out. He gives us a frightened smile—so? We give him huge hugs and stand back as a sobbing Kiyoko embraces him—the best reunion any of us have ever seen.

Later today, Kyle Bannon will turn back the clock as well. And if that wasn't call for celebration enough, the

FBI did in fact uncover the truth about his supposed hit-and-run accident. As he's said all along, it wasn't Kyle at all, but an inebriated civilian who had randomly driven near the naval base and hit an innocent bystander that night. Which means Kyle is about to savor two joyous reunions of his own—the first with his Navy SEAL team and the second, and most important, with his wife and daughter. Both of whom we'll meet at our wedding next month.

We give Louis a while to recover, and then it's my turn. I start toward the capsule, then look back at Louis and Dr. Layton.

"Ten, not twenty," I say.

Neither one understands, but Janine does. She moves toward me.

"Morgan, what are you doing?"

"Janine, listen to me. Do you know how happy I am to get any of these years back?"

"So take them!"

"I am, just not all of them."

"You're doing this for me, aren't you?"

"What's wrong with that?"

"Everything. You're worried people will think I've robbed the cradle if I'm married to a man ten years younger than me. But do you think I care about any of that? Did you care when it was the other way around all this time? I appreciate the gesture, but you have to do this. And that's that."

I should know by now that when the formidable Janine says "that's that," then that is indeed that. I shake my head in one last attempt to change her mind, but she'll have none of it.

"Besides," Janine says with a big smile, "just keeping up with me the rest of your life will age you at *least* ten years anyway."

I smile, give her a kiss, look over to my friends beaming at me, and say to Janine, "Lucky for you, I always preferred older women."

I step into the capsule. Time to go back. Time to start over. Time to surge forward.

I'm shaking both with excitement and trepidation as the capsule closes and a fine mist is sprayed within. Just like at Loomis, multi-colored lights engulf the capsule as it begins gliding down the magnetic track. But then I realize I'm not alternately boiling and freezing as I was the last time, and there's no deep rumbling sound either. It's all rather peaceful in a way.

After a minute or so, the capsule comes to a stop and opens. Dr. Layton helps me out, and I look at everyone's faces and wait for a reaction. What if they start screaming? But then I'm greeted by the biggest smiles I've ever seen. They guide me to a mirror and I nervously look myself over. My God. I'm young again. Gone are the telltale signs of middle age—the salt-and-pepper hair is dark again, the extra pounds and beginnings of a second chin are gone. My vision and hearing are fully restored. I even seem taller.

I'm not ashamed to admit that I start to cry—tears of joy, naturally, but also tears of cathartic relief. I never dared dream this day would come. The day I can truly and finally put the ordeal of TimeLock behind me. Lonny shot point blank. The cabin burning down. Twenty years of my life stolen. Running from the law. Fearing I would end up like so many of those unfortunate TimeLock prisoners. Putting Janine's life and career on the firing line time and time again. Subjecting my poor mother to such constant torment. Almost being killed by Loder and Colby more times than I can count. The loss of Yoshi's young friends at the Hakone lab. Foolishly allowing myself to be kidnapped by Prescott's men. Myra Winters. Sloane Whalen. Carter Prescott. Sergei Baranov.

But as these memories wash over me for what seems like minutes, yet is really only seconds, I also remember the good that has come from all this as well. Janine most of all, of course. But also Louis, Kiyoko, and Yoshi. The genuine kindness and surprising strength of character of President Bartlett, the support and generosity of Walter Greene, the profound bravery of Kyle Bannon, the unhesitant leadership of President Ayres, the budding friendship of young Mikhail.

I give Janine a long hug, then do the same with Louis, Kiyoko, Yoshi, and even Dr. Layton. As we embrace, I realize that only Janine has ever seen me this age, just as I've never seen Louis as a much younger man. It's no wonder we all stare at each other for what seems like an eternity. The rare "Twilight Zone" with a happy ending.

Finally, Yoshi turns to me and Louis and says, "I'm so jealous."

"Jealous?" I ask. "Why? You're still the youngest one here."

Yoshi breaks into a big smile and says, "Not about you both being so much younger. About you both being so much thinner. Has anyone ever considered TimeLock as a diet?"

CHAPTER THIRTY-ONE

It's been a long but wonderful day—Louis and I getting all those years back, then a short time later watching Kyle go through successfully as well.

And then the happiest moment of all when Janine and I stopped by my mother's house to reveal our big news. Worried about building up her hopes in advance in case the process didn't work, I hadn't told her about Louis's breakthrough.

No wonder, then, she couldn't believe what she was seeing when she opened the door. Indeed, even after Janine explained to her what had happened, my mom continued to stare at me in stunned silence for a full minute. Until the silence was broken by the loudest scream of pure joy I've ever heard in my life.

One week from now, my mother will celebrate another joyous occasion and more tears of happiness are sure to flow that day as well—many of them my own, no doubt. You see, next week Grace Sharon Eberly will be a new mom again—this time when she begins the process of formally adopting a certain young Russian boy named Mikhail. Not out of pity, but out of love for a young man who's won over the hearts of virtually everyone he's met since arriving in the United States. It's also not lost on any of us that had I not met Mikhail and had he not told me precisely how his poor father succumbed to Baranov's unhinged experiments, Louis, Kyle, and I would never have regained the years TimeLock stole from us. Clearly, the universe meant for him to be in our lives.

The day after our processing at GenQuest Bio-Tech, Janine is at her office and I'm back where it all started, our family's little mountain cabin. Given that this is where I watched Lonny die, where Colby and his partner tried to kill me before burning the place to the ground, and where my ordeal with TimeLock started, my mother and I were more than ready to sell our cabin property and never look back.

Then I remembered how much this place meant to my father, and I realized that eradicating it from our lives would almost be like losing him all over again. Yes, I was hardly the nature lover he was, but we were never closer as a family than when we were here. And that's a level of closeness I want to be able to share with Janine and our children the rest of my life.

There's another reason we decided to rebuild our modest little mountain home away from home. It's here more than any other place where I feel closest to my dad. Which is why, with Janine's encouragement, I've come up here alone for a few hours alone a week before our wedding just to walk around, take in the majesty of the tall trees and crystal blue lake dotting the landscape and let my father know how well I'm doing.

Strolling around the front of the cabin deep in thought, I don't speak out loud to my father, but am convinced he can somehow hear my thoughts and sense my feelings nonetheless. Most of all, I believe he knows how much I've gained despite—or perhaps because of—the ordeals I've been through since that fateful night when I asked Lonny to meet me up here.

Because the truth is, although Louis gave me my twenty years back, I still feel two decades older than I did before TimeLock. In a good way. As I told you before, I'm not sure I would recognize or particularly like the twenty-three-year-old Morgan Eberly anymore. In ways I'll probably never completely understand, this entire experience—this wild, nerve-wracking, terrifying, and at times seemingly hopeless experience—has made me a better person. More compassionate. More thoughtful. More patient. More responsible. And more ready to be worthy of a remarkable woman like Janine Price. How I wish you could meet her, Dad.

I cry for a minute, but the tears aren't unwelcome; they're cathartic and strangely comforting. As if my father is telling me to get the crying out of my system and get back to the business of living and to a future I now know will be filled with love, warmth, and happiness.

And then, this I do say out loud because I've never meant anything more: "I love you, Dad."

CHAPTER THIRTY-TWO

Back at our condo that evening, I tell Janine about my visit to the cabin and open a bottle of wine. I pour a glass then am about to pour another one but Janine gestures—none for her. We sit down and it's obvious she has something on her mind.

"What a week this has been," she says. "I'm so happy for you."

"I'm so happy for *us*," I respond.

"Which makes what I'm about to say all the more ironic."

Oh dear Lord—she's breaking up with me. I knew my life was going too well. Maybe being with a younger man is scaring her off after all. I shouldn't have listened to her about getting all twenty years back. I can barely speak, but manage a tentative, "What is it?"

"The thing is—this time it's *my* appearance that's about to change, and I hope you're okay with it."

"What do you mean your appearance?"

"I mean I'm going to look very different for a while." She pauses for a few seconds, then adds, "For nine months, to be exact."

Oh my God! Janine thought I'd be upset but the truth is, I've actually never been happier! I break into a huge smile and give my very relieved wife-to-be a hug that seems to go on forever.

"I thought we were being careful, but I must have . . ."

"You don't have to explain. This is the best news ever. Unless, of course, Walter is the father."

Janine smiles, shakes her head at my dumb joke, and says, "Are you sure? You just got your life back, we're not even married yet, and now—"

"And now I get to share it with you and our baby. Just one favor to ask you."

"What's that?" a beaming Janine asks.

"If it's a boy, I'd like to name him after my dad."

"I'll go one better. How about naming him after your father *and* your soon-to-be stepbrother?"

"Jackson Michael Eberly. Sounds like a business tycoon already."

"I was thinking it sounds more like an FBI Director, actually. But we have plenty of time to find out."

"I don't know about that," I say with a smile. "Children grow up really fast these days. Look at me, I went from being a dopey kid to a middle-aged man in about three minutes."

"Which reminds me. I kinda miss the salt-and-pepper hair."

"I'll work on it. How about my double chin? You miss that too?"

"Nah," she says with a big smile. "It was starting to get a little . . . old."

"Very funny."

We kiss and I give Janine another long hug. And then I just stare at her with an incredulous smile on my face. Because how could I not? Somehow, in some way, fate has decreed that this amazing woman who put her career and her life on the line for me so many times is about to become my wife and the mother of my child. Whether I deserve such a joyous fate, I can't be sure. But I'll spend the rest of my life trying to be worthy of it.

Because even though TimeLock almost made that life short and quick, now we get to live it the way it was meant to be lived.

Nice and slow.

THE END

ABOUT THE AUTHORS

An award-winning novelist and screen-writer, Howard Berk's credits include memorable episodes of such classic TV series as *Columbo*, *Mission: Impossible* and *The Rockford Files*, as well as the feature film, *Target*, starring Gene Hackman and Matt Dillon.

Peter Berk has written six novels, three TV pilots and a dozen screenplays, including several with his father which became the basis for the *TimeLock* series of novellas. Peter and his family live in Southern California.

IngramElliott Publishing

IngramElliott is an award-winning independent publisher with a mission to bring great stories to light in print and on-screen. We publish stories with a unique voice that will translate well into film and television. Visit us at www.ingramelliott.com for more information.

Our IngramElliott imprint features full-length fiction and non-fiction titles designed with the book lover in mind.

Our IE Snaps! imprint features novella-length fiction in popular genres that are designed for a quick read on the go.